WILY WRITERS
PRESENTS

# TALES
# OF
# NIGHTMARES

The *Wily Writers Presents* Anthology Series

## Tales of Dread
edited by Lisa Morton

## Tales of Nightmares
edited by Loren Rhoads

## Tales of Evil
edited by Angel Leigh McCoy
and Alison J. McKenzie

## Tales of Darkness
edited by Yvonne Navarro

## Tales of Foreboding
edited by E.S. Magill
and Bill Bodden

## Tales of Shadows
edited by Weston Ochse

WILY WRITERS
PRESENTS

# TALES
# OF
# NIGHTMARES

EDITED BY LOREN RHOADS

Dark Fiction Masterminds
2022

# WILY WRITERS PRESENTS: TALES OF NIGHTMARES

Edited by Loren Rhoads.
Cover and interior design by Rick Pickman.
Interior layout by Automatism Press.

First edition

ISBN: 9781735187679
ISBN (ebook): 9781735187686

Library of Congress Control Number: 2022912453


Printed in the United States of America.

Automatism Press
PO Box 12308
San Francisco, CA 94112 USA
www.automatismpress.com

https://wilywriters.net/

# Contents

*Introduction*.................................................................. *1*

*La Japonesa* by Lisa Morton.......................................... *3*

*Into the Quiet* by Alison J. McKenzie........................ *14*

*The Dark Watchers* by E.S. Magill............................. *20*

*Recall* by Yvonne Navarro........................................... *41*

*Twenty Questions* by Jennifer Brozek......................... *51*

*The Haunting of Mrs. Poole* by Angel Leigh McCoy.............. *69*

*Glue and the Art of Supermodel Maintenance*
by Weston Ochse............................................................ *89*

*Elle a Vu un Loup* by Loren Rhoads ........................ *92*

*The House on River Road* by Bill Bodden .............. *108*

# Introduction

## Loren Rhoads

I have the honor of being in several writers groups with Lisa Morton, former president of the Horror Writers Association and award-winning author of an ever-growing number of books on ghosts, Halloween, and zombies, as well as short stories, novels, and podcasts. Lisa was talking one night about these anthologies she had appeared in, alongside John Palisano, Eric J. Guignard, Rena Mason, and Kate Jonez. Each of them edited one book in the *Strange Tales of the Macabre* series, then each had a story in all five books. I was fascinated by the concept: sort of a round robin set of anthologies.

Then last year, Angel Leigh McCoy founded the Wily Writers collective, in which a bunch of writers—not all of them horror writers—support and encourage each other's work. I had a brainstorm: why didn't we put together some anthologies by the Wily Writers, to draw more attention to the group and showcase what we can do?

By the end of the first meeting of interested editors in January 2022, we'd hashed out the parameters of the series, chosen titles, and set deadlines. After that, it was just a matter of assembling the stories.

Lisa's book, *Tales of Dread*, was the first in the series. It came out in June 2022, a scant six months from when the idea first coalesced. This book—*Nightmares*—is the second in the series of six. The other four should appear more or less monthly for the rest of this year.

To say I am excited to participate in this series of anthologies would understate it. I am overjoyed to think that the idea I pitched to Angel in December last year is coming to such glorious and immediate fruition.

When we were batting around themes for the books, I was immediately drawn to *Nightmares*. It's safe to say that I really like nightmares. I find them thoroughly fascinating. How can imaginary pictures in my head cause such intense physical responses: the pounding heart, the ragged breaths, the muscle aches from running so hard or freezing so still as I hide?

When my kid was little, she was a sleepwalker. Either she would wake up calling my name or, worse, she would roam the house, eyes open but unfocused, terrified but unable to talk. Nightmares are a stage that all kids go through, as they encounter the outer world. Some of us never get past it.

Personally, I have a *lot* of nightmares, but I don't think of myself as suffering from them. I think of them as fuel for my imagination. I see them as inspirations. Prompts, one might say.

While these pages contain the odd hallucination or vision from beyond, you'll find no dream sequences here. These stories are designed to induce nightmares.

Dear reader, I don't want to wish you sweet dreams. For you, I wish inspiring nightmares.

# La Japonesa

## Lisa Morton

*Nekomusume.*

Amanda looked up from the strange word scrawled in her notepad and rolled the syllables around on her tongue, trying to imagine the correct pronunciation. She knew enough about Japanese to guess that one or more of the middle vowels might be essentially silent, but beyond that she had no idea.

*Jon would probably know just how to say it—or at least he would tell me how wrong I am,* she thought, while making a small grimace. Somehow the grimace was as close as she got to a smile these days.

*Nekomusume.* Beside that word was another one, equally exotic: *yokai.*

She read over her notes again: "*Yokai* = supernatural spirits in Japanese mythology. *Nekomusume* = a *yokai* that's a cat-woman. *La Japonesa* = *nekomusume.*"

Amanda took another sip of her flavored iced tea and looked up, scanning the street from where she sat on a concrete bench under the awning of a cheap taco stand in the bowels of the San Gabriel Valley. The only other customer was seated two tables away, a large man of indeterminate ethnicity tucking into a greasy taco as if it was his last meal.

In this area, it could well be.

She shifted on the hard plastic bench, wishing she were somewhere else. It was hot and smoggy and she didn't belong here, on the other end of L.A. from her safe university enclave. Her blouse was sticking to her skin and she was suddenly aware of how far away she'd parked. She should have been back in an air-conditioned classroom, telling a bunch of disinterested college kids that there was more to American folklore than Paul Bunyan and his blue ox.

At least she didn't have to come home to Jon. Her quiet, empty guesthouse, tucked away in a canyon above the campus, was better than the expensive three-bedroom estate full of the noise of failure.

It was now a quarter after three and she was starting to think she'd been the victim of a joke. The two kids who'd claimed to have seen

Southern California's *La Japonesa* (and who'd agreed to meet her here, at three) hadn't showed, and Amanda could imagine them right now, hanging with their friends, laughing about the lady professor they'd punked.

But that didn't explain why they'd given an interview to the local newspaper, the *El Monte Tribune*.

Amanda looked up and noticed the big man had finished his taco and was staring at her, with something halfway between open hostility and sardonic amusement. She felt a gush of adrenaline, pure fight-or-flight instinct, and decided to leave.

Provided she could.

She was just closing up her notebook when the throb of a deep engine announced a fresh arrival in the taco stand's lot. The car was a new SUV, black, an expensive model, and Amanda wondered who could afford a car like that in this rundown area of Southern California. Jon had gotten their SUV in the divorce settlement; on her salary, she could barely afford a six-year-old sedan.

The doors opened and two Latino kids got out. They were dressed in the uniform of their generation—baggy jeans, designer sneakers, sports team jerseys—and they nodded as they saw her.

"Hey, you Miz Houston?" said the taller boy.

Amanda nodded and relaxed slightly. "Yes. You must be Tommy and Rafael."

"That's us."

Amanda was gratified to see that the large man gave up watching her and slunk off.

The two kids ordered drinks, then joined her at the table. "So you wanna know about *La Japonesa*, huh?" Rafael asked her. He was smaller than Tommy, with an acne-scarred face and at least three rings on each hand.

"Yes, among other things."

Tommy squinted at her. "What other things?"

"I'm writing a book called *Folklore in Transition*. There's a lot of local stuff in it."

Rafael said, "You mean more weird shit like the cat-lady?"

Amanda nodded. "Right. But let's talk about what you saw." Then, hoping she'd copied their accents, she added, "*La Japonesa*."

Their grins vanished, and in that instant Amanda believed they'd seen *something*.

Tommy hunched forward, narrowing his bulky shoulders. "It was pretty fuckin' creepy—Oh, sorry."

"That's okay," Amanda said. She pulled out her phone, set it between them. "Is it okay if I record this?"

The boys shrugged. She started the audio recording app as she asked, "Had you heard of *La Japonesa* before?"

The boys exchanged a quick glance and Rafael played with his rings. "Sure. Everybody's heard of her—the cat-lady up in the hills. Sometimes she takes out a dog or somethin'. Last year when that hiker was mauled, they said it was a mountain lion, but we know it was her. *La Japonesa*."

Amanda made a mental note to check the hiker story before asking, "What else had you heard?"

Rafael answered, "My *tía* told me that she was, like, this spirit brought over from Japan by these Spanish traders, and she was really pissed off at being brought here, like two hundred years ago, so she took this form of a cat-lady and killed people every once in a while."

"Did you know other people who'd seen her?"

Another quick look, then Tommy said, "No."

"So tell me about what happened when you saw her."

Rafael leaned forward, excited. "It was two weeks ago. Real hot night, and me and Tommy, we couldn't sleep, so we decided to go up into the hills—"

Amanda cut in: "At night?"

The two boys looked mildly nervous, and when Tommy answered, Amanda thought he was lying. "Yeah, we...uh...go up there sometimes to...y'know...just chill."

Amanda nodded, trying to look as if she believed them. "So this one night..."

"Yeah," Rafael went on, "we're up there and it's about three in the morning, and we hear something just below us, and then we see these eyes, you know, shining. Like a cat's eyes, yellow with slit pupils, but big, and we're like, Ah, shit, it's a mountain lion! But then we get our flashlight pointed at it, and there's a human face around the eyes—"

Tommy added, "—and it's a woman, and she's beautiful, but she's got these big ears that stick up, like a cat's, and it looks like she's even got more than one tail."

"What happened next?"

"She fuckin' growled at us," Rafael said, and Amanda thought the glint of fear in his expression was probably real. "And we ran. I mean, we just took off, figurin' the whole way that this thing would catch us and tear us up any second, but...it didn't."

Tommy twisted the straw in his drink. "But the next morning, they found a dead dog up there, torn apart. And I'm thinkin' that fuckin' dog saved our lives, man—she went after it instead of us. Otherwise we might not be here talkin' to you."

Amanda asked, "Do you think you could take me to where you saw her?"

The look of dismay and—what, deceit?—that passed between the two boys was obvious. "No, we can't do that," said Tommy.

"Why not?"

"Because…we're afraid to go up there now."

Rafael said, "Besides, we were…uh…wasted that night. We couldn't really find it again anyway."

Amanda closed the recording app and looked up at them. "Okay, I think that's it. Thanks for your time. Feel free to text me if you think of anything else."

"Oh, there is one other thing…" Tommy added.

Amanda paused halfway off the bench and waited.

The two boys exchanged a look before Rafael snorted and turned away, leaving Tommy to go on nervously: "I…since that night, I've been…dreaming about her. Like, these dreams feel real, like she's there all the time now."

Amanda stared at him for a beat, not knowing how to respond.

"So are we, like, gonna be in your book?" asked Rafael.

That broke Amanda's paralysis and she turned away. "I'll let you know."

She left without looking back.

"They were lying."

"I'm not so sure."

Sam paused, forkful of salad halfway to his mouth. "C'mon, Mandy—they're publicity hounds."

Amanda sipped her tea and glanced around the crowded university cafeteria. "Maybe, but I think they really saw something up there."

Her friend set down his fork and looked her straight in the eye. Sam West was older than Amanda, with unashamed gray in his beard and an air of confidence; he had long ago achieved the tenure she was still struggling for. "I know how important this book is to you, and yes—you need to publish, it'll boost your shot at tenure, it'll help you recover from the divorce, all of that…but don't tell me you actually believe any of this."

"No, but I'd like to." Amanda pushed her cup aside, warming to the subject. "You remember the story, right?"

Sam made a wry face. "Of course."

Of course—it'd been a stupid question. Sam's book *Crying Women and Cat Spirits: Mexican Folklore North of the Border* had inspired Amanda's interest in *La Japonesa*.

Amanda continued, "Okay, I know you do, but just hear me out: So the story starts in Mexico, as a traditional folktale about a legendary cat-woman who's brought over from Japan by Spanish traders in the 17th century, right? Her spirit is trapped in an urn that they carelessly leave beside a cactus patch. She finally escapes the urn and becomes a vengeful monster, a cat with four tails that kills anyone who comes near the urn. At some point, the immigrants come north over the border to America and bring the story with them, and now *La Japonesa* is still haunting the Southern California hills three centuries later, so—Sam, I think this is the best example in California of a traditional folktale that's still alive, still evolving."

Sam nodded, considering. "I can see that."

"I checked the news of the mauled hiker that those kids mentioned, and it was real—they never did catch whatever killed that hiker. And all the eyewitness reports say she's beautiful…"

Sam laughed. "Yeah, okay—I'd like an eyeful of her, too."

"And she's the perfect symbol of Southern California folklore—a blend of different cultures. A mix of ghost, human, and animal. The ultimate icon of the Los Angeles melting pot."

Sam chewed for a second then said, "Just reassure me of one thing: That this isn't some midlife crisis thing where the woman hurt in the messy divorce fixates on a strong female figure."

Amanda laughed. But she didn't really smile.

The next day, Amanda took a hike into the foothills above El Monte.

She wore jeans, a sweatshirt, and heavy hiking boots, and she tucked her violet-dyed hair up under a baseball cap that Jon had left behind. She started up a trail about four in the afternoon, moving from sage and cactus, gravel and dust, up to manzanita and scrub pine and boulder. Although she saw small clusters of trash that might have been either stoners' hangouts or homeless camps, she encountered no one else. At one point she found a sturdy six-foot length of tree limb and turned it into a walking staff, although its heft in her hands made her feel safer for other reasons.

She knew it was unwise to stay in the hills after dark (she wouldn't have wanted to encounter Tommy and Rafael up here, she thought with some irony), that there was no point to it…but all of the witnesses to *La Japonesa* had reported sighting her between the hours of two and four a.m., and Amanda thought she knew why. In Japanese mythology, that period (which was a single hour in the old Japanese method of reckoning time) was called "the hour of the ox." It was a time when *yokai* were traditionally easiest to see. *Yokai*—spirits—like *La Japonesa*.

So she found a shelter made by a large boulder to the back and a patch of grassy earth beneath it, spread a blanket, and sat down to wait.

The first hour after sunset was unnerving; Amanda jumped at every skitter and bird-cry. As night deepened, she found herself strangely soothed by the panorama of the L.A. cityscape lit up below her. The evening was warm, the air clearer at even this slight altitude, and Amanda found a contemplative space she hadn't known in some time.

She thought about her book; she'd been working on it for over a year and had hundreds of pages of notes but little finished text. She contemplated her classes. Her friends. Her failed marriage.

And she didn't much like what she saw.

She was in the middle of a life that hadn't been extraordinary. She was nearly forty and had realized no dreams. Achieved no serious goals. Had little to show. The day Jon had told her he was leaving, he'd called her "a serious underachiever."

She thought he was probably right.

The lights below were redolent of a glittering history that Amanda had never really claimed; she'd tried to embrace the stories and adventures, but they'd always felt too far outside of her mundane reality. She wanted to be special, part of something bigger than herself…but neither marriage nor academic life had provided solace. She shivered and realized that even this expedition had been reduced to practical considerations—would she be able to find her way back in the dark? Did she have anything she could use for warmth…or a weapon? When she finally checked the time on her phone, she was surprised to see it was after three in the morning.

The Hour of the Ox.

Just as she lowered the phone, she heard it: a low, guttural snarl somewhere off in the dark.

Amanda froze, all thoughts of Jon and failings abruptly shut down.

A small cascade of gravel, somewhere off to her right. Maybe a hundred feet.

Amanda drew herself up against the boulder, grabbed at the large stick she'd acquired, holding it out before her. She jumped as more skittering pebbles sounded. Whatever was out there, it was circling her.

Getting closer.

Should she turn on the flashlight, see if she could spot it? Or would that just make her an easier target?

Another growl, this time to her left. It had gone around her 180 degrees. It could obviously already see, or scent, her. The flashlight probably wouldn't make much difference.

She turned it on, pointing it towards the location of the last noise.

The beam fell on glowing cat eyes.

At first Amanda felt a thrill, exhilaration. Then she saw the face around the eyes—the tawny pelt, large wet nose, long teeth.

A mountain lion.

Amanda cried out and involuntarily swung the branch in a semi-circle. The huge cat snarled, turned, and fled.

Amanda sat huddled against the rock, panting, her heart thundering; she felt pain in her left hand and realized she'd scraped her skin against the rock and was bleeding. She was sure the predator would smell her blood/hear her terror and return, that the last thing she'd feel would be its hot breath in her face as its claws caused her flesh to sing in agony.

The flashlight shook in her hands, the beam jittery as it raked the high desert landscape around her. After fifteen minutes, the light died and Amanda shoved it back in her knapsack. She'd have to use her phone from here on. Its charge should hold long enough for her to reach her car.

The sun was just starting to rise as she stumbled the last of the way to her Kia, staggered in, locked the doors, and then let herself shake for a few moments.

When all that was left was emptiness, she started up the car and drove home.

Two days later, Sam showed her a story in the paper about two kids in El Monte who'd been caught growing marijuana at a location hidden in the hills. They'd had roughly 2,000 plants up there, plants they'd grown with water hijacked from a city water reserve.

The boys were identified as Rafael Gomez, 18, and Tomas Mendoza, 19.

"Looks like they made up the *La Japonesa* story to scare off people from going up there and finding their little rancho. Didn't work, I guess," Sam said.

"No, I guess it didn't," Amanda answered.

"How's the book coming?"

"Oh…well, I can finish out the chapter on the cat-woman now."

Sam smiled. "Yeah. Are you going to title it '*La Japonesa*, Guardian of Pot Farms'?"

Amanda hadn't told Sam (or anyone else) about her little overnight stay in the hills, so she knew he wouldn't understand if she told him that her own private joke title for that chapter was "*La Japonesa*, Mountain Lyin'."

And the subtitle would have been, "The Night I Lost the Last of My Hope."

A week later, Amanda received a text from Tommy: "U probly know we got busted. But we didnt lie about La Japonesa—we really saw her. And Im still having dreams."

Then Amanda read the last line of the email and felt a tremor race along her spine: "And she knows about you."

Amanda's job would be up for review in a month.

Enrollment in the university's folklore studies program was down, even with the minor celebrity status of Sam West, who'd once hit a local bestseller list with one of his books. Amanda knew she needed to show something—a manuscript, at least, even if there was no publishing deal yet.

She tried to work seriously on *Folklore in Transition*. She started collating her notes, trying to lose herself in stories of the supposed curse on Griffith Park. Of the Roosevelt Hotel in Hollywood, haunted by the ghosts of celebrities. Of animals predicting earthquakes, and Mexican *botanicas* that cured with herbs and spirits, and the 1930s prospector G. Warren Shufelt and his search for the serpent people's tunnels of gold beneath the city.

But mostly she came back to *La Japonesa*. What had once been a symbol of the way L.A. melded varying cultures had now become emblematic of the city's ability to shatter illusion.

Summer was running late this year—it was mid-October, and the nighttime temperatures were still in the 80s. Amanda's guesthouse, nestled against a canyon wall, sheltered by a chaotic mix of hibiscus and palm, stayed cooler than the house she'd shared with Jon had, but it was still warm enough at night that she left the windows open while she worked.

She was pulling late-nighters recently, a lot of them spent staring at a laptop screen and a bewildering mess of hundreds of pages of scribbled notes. Tonight she'd actually managed to type a few paragraphs, but now it was 2 a.m. and she felt her attention span slipping away.

She was about to turn off the laptop when a phrase caught her eye: The Hour of the Ox.

It was after 2 a.m. *Synchronicity in action*, she thought. *Jung would be proud.*

She turned away—and gasped as she saw something glittering in the darkness just outside her open windows:

A pair of yellow eyes, with cat pupils.

*Jesus, a mountain lion here?*

She froze, staring hard into the darkness, trying to think of something she could use as a weapon, or as protection—

The eyes moved, then, towards the window, until they were just past the screen, and that was when Amanda saw the human nose and mouth.

*La Japonesa* looked in at her.

Amanda was terrified. This wasn't revelation, or transcendence, but pure, heart-pounding fear. The hair on the back of her neck prickled and her fingers curled into fists.

She wanted to yell at the thing, to send it away, but she could utter no sounds beyond a slight croak.

*It found me*, she thought, and then remembered that night on the hill, her scraped palm: *Because of my blood.*

The creature at the window lifted a limb. It was the length and structure of a human arm, but was covered in a short, silky golden fur and had claws on the ends of the fingers, claws that unsheathed as Amanda watched. The cat-woman gently drew the claws across the surface of the screen, and the mesh parted like a lover's lips.

She pulled the screen apart—and then leapt up to the sill and over, into the room.

Amanda didn't move. She watched, paralyzed, knowing that even if she could get up and run she'd never outrace this thing. It stood on two powerful, lightly furred back legs, and had four long, thin tails.

Four. In Japanese, the word for "four"—*shi*—sounded like the word for "death."

But if *La Japonesa* intended to murder Amanda, it wouldn't happen quickly. Instead the cat-woman peered at Amanda for a long moment, her almond-shaped, wine-colored eyes expressing great interest, even affection.

*She knows*, thought Amanda. *It's impossible, but…she knows I'm writing about her.*

*La Japonesa* moved towards her.

Amanda smelled a powerful animal musk and drew back, although there was nowhere to go. The cat-woman seemed to sense Amanda's fear, and her face (the small part of Amanda that could still articulate thought, *My God, she is exquisite*) subtly shifted, her lovely pink mouth drawing slowly up.

She took another step, and another, until she stood a few feet away, and then she slowly raised one hand/paw, a single claw extended. Amanda flinched as the paw approached her face, but she couldn't stop watching as the downy-pelted fingers reached for her forehead, gently slid down her face—

—and then she felt the pain as the claw pierced her cheek.

She cried out and did close her eyes now, not wanting to see where the claw went next, expecting to feel the pain, her flesh being torn open, the smell of her blood and its heat as it spilled from her, her death happening as she felt every nerve twitch and pulse…

But it didn't happen.

She finally opened her eyes again, just in time to see *La Japonesa* jump to the sill, turning back to look at Amanda a last time before she vanished into the night.

Amanda was shaking badly, her legs felt nerveless, but she managed to get up, slam all the windows shut and check the locks, then stagger into the bathroom. The cut on her right cheek was no more than two inches long, but it was deep, and Amanda knew it would leave a permanent scar.

She'd been marked.

As she watched a gauze pad held up to the wound redden, she knew she'd see that scar for the rest of her life, every morning when she looked into a mirror. Students and friends and lovers would see it and ask how she'd gotten it. Most she'd lie to, tell them she'd been careless with a cat.

A few she'd answer truthfully.

She thought she'd never see *La Japonesa* again, or anything else like her, but whenever she saw that narrow white ridge on her face, she would *know*, know that she'd been allowed into the mysteries, that she was now a part of something vast and old and untamed.

Amanda smiled.

## ABOUT THE AUTHOR

Lisa Morton is a screenwriter, author of nonfiction books, and prose writer whose work was described by the American Library Association's *Readers' Advisory Guide to Horror* as "consistently dark, unsettling, and frightening." She is a six-time winner of the Bram Stoker Award®, the author of four novels and over 150 short stories, and a world-class Halloween and paranormal expert. Her recent releases include *Night Terrors & Other Tales*, *Weird Women 2* (co-edited with Leslie S. Klinger), and *Calling the Spirits: A History of Seances*; her latest short stories appeared in *Best American Mystery Stories 2020*, *The Year's Top Tales of Time and Space*, *Final Cuts: New Tales of Hollywood Horror and Other Spectacles*, and *Classic Monsters Unleashed*. She has appeared on The History Channel, Discovery+, and The Military Channel, and can be heard every week on the popular podcast *Ghost Magnet With Bridget Marquardt*. Forthcoming is *Haunted Tales: Classic Stories of Ghosts and the Supernatural* (co-edited with Leslie S. Klinger). Lisa lives in Los Angeles and online at www.lisamorton.com.

# Into the Quiet

Alison J. McKenzie

Shana poured another glass of wine while the baby screamed in the other room.

*The baby.* Not "Nell," no, not the name Shana had argued with Ryan for months over, only to have him leave right after she was born. Just "the baby." Shana had noticed it creeping into her thoughts, this abstraction. This dehumanization.

It wasn't that she didn't love Nell. Not that at all. It was the shrieking—the incessant, high-pitched howling—through the morning, through the afternoon, through the evening, into the night hours, through to dawn, and over again.

*Maybe this is what going insane feels like.*

The wine—non-alcoholic, an empty gesture, a routine, a placebo—tasted both too sweet and too bitter. Mid-sip, Shana suddenly burst into tears, choking on the mouthful of liquid.

She was so, so tired.

So tired it didn't feel real. So tired, she could lean her back against the wall and melt into the plaster, down into the floor, and become part of the house. So tired that crying seemed like all she was capable of. Crying, drinking wine, checking the baby.

*Checking Nell.*

And she did check her, again.

Even with her face red and scrunched up, Nell looked like a tiny little angel. She'd gotten pretty so fast. When she'd been born, she was a normal newborn, with a too-big head and Yoda eyes, but she was a cherub now. When she cried, she kicked her feet out, and they were the cutest toes.

Watching them now, twitching and kicking under the blanket, an occasional sock peeking out from under the lavender knit, Shana felt a tug at her heart. Yes, she did love Nell. So, so much. And those few moments when Nell was calm, when she suckled, when she giggled, the love was as overwhelming as the exhaustion.

Shana was tired, that's all.

She wiped her tears with her sleeve and sipped her fake wine, doing her usual check with her off hand. No fever. Not hungry. Not hot, not cold. No scratches. Just shrieking.

"Hey," she murmured. "What's the matter, sugar?"

But Nell didn't answer, couldn't answer, although maybe the crying *was* an answer, one Shana couldn't understand.

Something gray swam past the corner of her vision. Hallucinations, again. Wisps of spiderwebs, shifting inky blobs, dancing lights... Sometimes the phantoms were more solid, like a man standing in her kitchen talking to her but speaking backwards, and she tried to ask him to slow down or stop talking but her lips were too heavy. The longer she went with so little sleep, the more real the hallucinations became. One night, she'd been sure a woman lay in bed next to her, singing a soundless lullaby and promising that Shana could rest, that the specter would watch the baby, that everything would be all right. Shana had wept then, too, from sheer relief, that someone was there to take over. That she could get some sleep. But it wasn't real. When her head cleared, she was still alone, and the baby— *the baby*—was still crying.

She turned to look at the amorphous shape, knowing it wouldn't be there when she did, that it was just a sliver of nothingness conjured up in her own mind. As she peered toward the hall, she met the eyes of someone who was standing there, who shouldn't be there, who was looking directly at her.

Then they were gone.

With a cry, Shana bolted into the hallway, but she found it empty. If anyone had run from her, she would have heard their footsteps.

Just another wisp.

With a sigh, Shana returned to the nursery and pushed the door shut behind her. She crossed to the baby, felt her forehead again, and sank into the slouched, threadbare easy chair she'd dragged next to the crib some time before Ryan left. Back when he still lived here, he hadn't wanted the baby to sleep in the master bedroom, so they'd turned his office into the nursery—though he'd resented that, too.

Leaning her head back, Shana closed her eyes and let the crying turn to white noise. But she couldn't sleep, couldn't disconnect, couldn't unplug herself from that maternal part of her so acutely aware of Nell's distress.

"Am I a bad mother?" she asked the ceiling. The afternoon glow had taken on a copper hue. Shadows shifted above her as cars passed the window outside. The shadows became cats darting from wall to wall, then bats fluttering.

Then, silence.

She peered at the crib. Nell was breathing, making occasional murmuring noises. The baby had settled down.

Shana shut her eyes again and felt herself drifting off, lifting off, flying away into—

Another shriek. She jumped in her chair.

"Please stop," Shana wailed, her body wracking with sobs. "Please just tell me. Tell me what you need. I'll fix it, baby. I'll fix it. Just tell me. Then we can both sleep."

As her tears dried on her cheeks, she stared out into the empty hallway and imagined a parade of women in old-fashioned gowns following the trails of headlight beams along the wall.

"Didn't I close you?" she asked the door, but it didn't answer.

It took a Herculean effort to pull her heavy, heavy body from the chair and drag one foot after the other to the doorway. She closed the nursery door again, listened as it latched, felt it click in her hands.

"There," she told it. "Stay like that."

Nell had faded to unhappy whimpering.

Shana crossed to her, lifted her to her shoulder, and bounced up and down gently, making soothing noises. This poor child.

Nell pushed away from her, squirming until Shana put her back down. Shana stroked her little head.

"Want to go to the doctor again tomorrow?" she asked. "You want another new one? Someone who can help?"

Nell grumbled and opened her mouth to shriek again.

Shana raised both hands to her own forehead, as if pressure could dull the sound that seemed to reverberate off her skull. She was half tempted to retreat to the kitchen, pour more wine, but stopped short when she saw the door was open again.

She made a noise of surprise that couldn't be defined as a word. This time, she ran to the door and slammed it shut.

Either she was finally cracking, or someone really was in her house.

Her cell phone was far away, in the living room. She couldn't leave Nell alone in the nursery with someone in the house; nor would she bring the baby out of the room with her into possible danger.

She started toward the window, thinking of opening it up and shouting, but it had vanished. The wall was pastel yellow paint from floor to ceiling. Shana reached out a trembling hand to touch where the window should have been. Solid plaster met her fingertips.

Behind her, she heard the door creak open.

She snatched Nell from the crib and held her close to her chest. Though the baby struggled again, Shana did not let go.

In the easy chair, the man spoke backwards to her.

"Get out!" Shana snarled at him, but he wasn't there. The chair was empty.

The elegant women paraded down the hallway again, this time in reverse, like a film played backwards. The headlights they followed were also reversed, as though cars on the streets were backstepping the way they came, shining their lanterns through a window that wasn't there anymore.

"In my head," Shana whispered, but the words came out garbled and breathy, as if she'd forgotten how to talk.

The spectacle ended abruptly. Silence fell, so sharp and sudden, that Shana thought the whole world had stopped. She looked down; Nell was still screaming, but nothing came out of her mouth.

Shana closed her eyes and held the baby tighter: not so tight as to hurt her but tight enough that she imagined herself as a loving, impenetrable armor swallowing Nell up, a living barrier, a tree with branches that interwove and a root system so deep in the earth nothing could move it.

Softly, so softly, a lullaby came to her, sweet and beautiful.

"I know you," Shana said, and the shape of a woman settled in the air next to her.

"Shhhhhhh," the air cooed, though the lullaby did not cease or falter. "Shhhhhhhh."

"I'm so tired," Shana said. "I'm so tired and I don't know what's real." She roused herself and looked at the woman beside her, only to face empty air. In an instant, the sound came flooding back. The baby was crying. The lullaby was gone.

"Come back," Shana cried, but it was drowned out by little Nell in her arms.

The door was open again—no, there was no door, only a gaping hole into a hallway that looked like hers but went somewhere her own hallway didn't go. She could see flitting petticoats as figments of women fled down that hall, their feet kissing the hardwood without a sound, their shapes existing only in fragments of light.

Movement from the corner of her eye—the man, getting abruptly to his feet from the armchair, yelling at her so loudly she took a step back, but his words were still backwards and she could barely hear him over the siren wail of Nell.

"Stop," Shana blubbered, her voice noise amongst noise. "Stop, stop, stop, stop…"

She ran from him, clutching the screaming child to her breast. He grabbed at her as she tried to flee. For a moment, he had Ryan's face. She wrenched away from him and made for the missing hall.

Standing in the doorway was a woman who wasn't there, who smiled a sweet, sweet smile, and reached her arms out to take the baby. Her eyes were so kind. Shana felt a burst of relief and love. Without thinking, she handed Nell to her, as though the woman were her own mother, a rescuer from Heaven itself, offering to take her burden so that she can rest, rest...

Shana woke up.

The air was still. She could hear traffic outside, the air conditioner kicking on. So familiar, but something was so wrong.

At first, she couldn't understand where she was. It wasn't until she looked at the window, the window that had disappeared but was now back, the window that was in a white wall, not yellow, that the horror struck her.

Ryan's home office. The office he had not wanted to give up for the baby. There was the desk Shana had hauled to the garage herself, the oversized executive chair she had tossed down the stairs. The fan palm where the threadbare easy chair should be. The empty carpet where the crib should be.

Ryan's home office, which was no longer a nursery. Had never been a nursery.

Shana screamed and flew out of the room in a flurry of confusion. From the kitchen, a man came running. It was Ryan, apron draped over his neck, asking her what was wrong, and though he wasn't speaking backwards, he might as well have been.

There was no bassinet next to the sofa, no highchair—as of yet unused—pushed up against the dining room table. No trace of her. The night was silent. Painfully, painfully silent.

Shana sank to her knees, feeling as though something had been sucked out of her. Of Nell. Shana gasped for air, trying to sob but unable to breathe until something inside collapsed and she felt the tears, hot, stinging tears that ran down her face.

Ryan got down beside her, took her in his arms, and held her while she, alone, cried into the quiet of the house.

## ABOUT THE AUTHOR

Alison J. McKenzie is a writer and freelance editor. They worked in the video game industry for seven years, primarily as a game writer but also in web marketing. Currently they are a technical writer in the travel industry, based out of the greater Seattle area. In their free time, they write dark fiction in short and long form. See their published and upcoming projects at AlisonJMcKenzie.com.

Reach them at alison@alisonjmckenzie.com.

# The Dark Watchers

E.S. Magill

"No one knew who the Watchers were, nor where they lived, but it was better to ignore them and never to show interest in them. They did not bother one who stayed on the trail and minded his own business."

—John Steinbeck

"There's the exit for State Route 1," the woman riding shotgun said. She went by Jones. Of the three he was escorting into the Santa Lucia Mountain Range, she was younger, pretty in a steely way, ice blonde with Nordic blue eyes. She turned off the phone and stowed it in her Black Diamond jacket pocket.

"Done navigating?" Although he had assumed cell phone reception was de rigueur in every nook and cranny of California—how else were agents and managers supposed to stay in touch?—Kimball had learned that getting a signal along the coast was next to impossible. Jones gave him a forced grin. From the ditty bag between her feet, she pulled out a waterproof map. Damn. Kimball stopped smirking.

He stole a look in the rearview mirror at the two in the back seat: a middle-aged man and woman, neither remarkable, plain features and mousy brown hair. They could have been twins. The man's build was unassuming, lithe in fact, but when he shook Kimball's hand, he squeezed hard. This was the Smith Kimball had spoken with on the phone several weeks earlier. The woman beside Smith was Miller. Neither engaged him in small talk. Instead, they perused the books they brought with them, musty things that made Kimball turn the vent on high. Who brings books on a backpacking trip?

When he had met up with the three—that's how he thought of them, the three—at the airport, he first noticed that none wore jeans and their boots showed wear. Signs they weren't *hickers* and had more outdoor experience than they claimed. Their names made him nervous. Smith, Jones, and Miller—he would be damned if those were real. He worried they might be journalists out to write another exposé about him. Or maybe insurance investigators, which was more likely since they possessed pockets deep enough to fund this overpriced excursion. He would have to watch himself, and them, whoever they really were.

They drove south along the Pacific Coast Highway, passing through urban centers with the same big box stores and chain restaurants cloned from coast to coast and points in between. Kimball wrinkled his nose as if smelling something bad. It surprised him, however, at how quickly the Best Buys and Golden Arches dropped away as the Coast Highway opened up to mountains, valleys, and the Pacific coastline. Kimball had to give California credit for doing the impossible. Even though it was the most populous state, activism and legislation protected a whole swath of land between Monterey and Morro Bay. There wasn't a chain store or fast-food restaurant for over a hundred miles. No mass development at all. Homes and businesses—the few there were—remained discreet, camouflaged by nature.

The three took no notice of their surroundings. When he took clients out, especially those cloistered in cubicles from nine to five, they oohed-and-awed over every mountain peak and squirrel dashing across the road. The three hadn't commented on the beauty of the California coast even once. Kimball tried to impart local facts he researched for the trip, but none of the three showed any interest. Beside him, Jones propped her head against the window, napping. Smith and Miller in the back seat pored over those old books. Kimball checked another mark in the suspicious column. Perhaps agreeing to take on this trip wasn't such a great idea after all, but they lured him with an obscene amount of money.

Eventually, Kimball decided their silence was fine by him. Left alone with his thoughts was just the way he liked things. He had plenty to think about.

Two weeks earlier, he had been contemplating ending it all. His life had no purpose as far as he was concerned. Kimball had spent almost a year curled up on his living room couch, trying to feel as little as possible and lamenting his lost career as one of the premier professional backpackers in the world. Empty bottles of liquor blotted the surface of his coffee table, creating a relief map of intoxication. Piles of clipped articles from mangled magazines and newspapers littered the floor beneath the table. He had read and reread the articles until they resembled moths that had beaten themselves against light bulbs. Not a single article offered sympathy or consolation for the accident that had happened on his watch, just condemnation. His finances were decimated. Not only had his pro hiking business ended, but his sponsors abandoned him as if his curse would pass onto them. The hiking equipment line deal with REI died, leaving Kimball wondering if he wasn't better off that way, too.

Over the previous several years, he'd kept getting more clients who believed that because they recycled and drove an electric vehicle, they were nature experts. They treated mountain excursions like luxury resorts, refusing to believe nature came with teeth and claws and no conscience. On that last trip—the one that destroyed his whole life—his clients disobeyed almost every order he gave. They were slow to put up the tents, passing a flask around instead, and ended up soaked by a sudden thunderstorm. The eldest of them developed pneumonia and had to be airlifted out. Kimball told them not to feed the animals or trample vegetation, which they did anyway. He especially warned them not to wander away from camp, to stay in the company of his experienced guides. The image of what he found one morning kept flashing through his mind, unbidden and bloody. All the alcohol and self-abuse could not exorcise it away. Those people had been his responsibility and the media gave him a social lynching. Kimball let them. He packed away his equipment, took down his website, and hid from the world.

Then Smith called. Now here Kimball was, doing it one more time, even though he refused the stranger several times. Smith said they wanted him, only him. Kimball hung up the first time. The man persisted. His team wanted to hike the Santa Lucia Mountain Range in California. Kimball said definitely no. Never did California, never wanted to. California was for tourists. Millions of people visited places like Yosemite and Big Sur, making them no better than Bourbon Street or Times Square. For Kimball, nature was a personal experience, best done on an intimate level. On the third call, Smith put a number on his offer. Dollar signs wrestled with Kimball's guilt. This could be his comeback, his redemption.

Kimball allowed the two sides to brawl. In the end, guilt took the beating, and money won.

*But if it happened again...the bodies...*

Don't start, Kimball. Just don't start with that. Put it aside. Be here right now.

Even if his clients chose to ignore the natural beauty around them, Kimball felt bound to absorb every bit of it. He turned his attention to the ocean on his right. The water appeared as a flat mass clear to the horizon. On his left, mountains stood guard, seeming to protect the continent from being inundated by the ocean, but he knew it was all deception. The mountains and a sizeable chunk of California were not part of the continental United States. Here, the Pacific Plate and the North American

Plate were smashing, grinding, sliding against one another. The Pacific Plate's primary mass lay submerged beneath dark waters. Those underwater mountains had pushed out of their watery depths like some ridged-back sea creature five million years earlier, transforming the coastline. The result was the Santa Lucia Range, a geologically young range where wind and water had yet to wear down her jagged peaks into rounded scoops and turn steep canyons into salad bowl valleys. They would be hiking a rugged landscape Mother Nature had yet to temper.

Of course, modern man arrived and needed ready access to all that beauty. Thinking they were godlike, manipulating geology to serve their purposes, they hewed the Pacific Coast Highway into those mountains. Sometimes the road was nothing more than a ledge on the rim of the world. In those places, mountains from time to time shook off a hoary avalanche of dirt and rock, blocking passage, reminding man who truly ruled.

Just as Kimball's view of the ocean became tranquil and commonplace, PCH meandered away from the coast, inland. It bisected valleys—verdant pastures stretching eastward—the road returning to the coast with more pastureland overlooking the ocean. Cows grazed contentedly on those cliff-hugging fields. It was virginal land that made developers weep with envy: to think only dull-witted ungulates had access to all that expensive real estate.

"Do you think any cows have ever gone over the edge?" Smith asked.

The two women chuckled.

"Sorry about that, Kimball," Smith said.

The fucked-up comment startled Kimball from his reverie. Was the bastard actually referencing the accident? He said nothing, just made another tick on his mental chart.

Traffic turned bumper to bumper at the famed Bixby Bridge. From the vantage point of a boat, it was less a bridge and resembled more a portal between worlds. Vehicles lined both sides of the road as sightseers left their cars to snap pictures of the bridge, the mountains, and the waves crashing at the base of the cliffs. Kimball understood the emotions a place like this evoked, but all the damned people scampering about to pose at the cliff's edge just cheapened the experience. Kimball accelerated once he cleared the span.

"Watch out."

He braked hard, snapping everyone forward like rubber bands.

A man darted out in front of Kimball's Suburban. He didn't even acknowledge the squeal of tires or the bumper inches from his thigh but just kept heading for the other side of the road, his phone held out in front of him.

"Goddamn moron," Kimball muttered. The incident supported his disdain for touristy places. He continued driving.

"It's going to rain, really rain," Miller said. "Then all these people will be gone."

"Yeah, doesn't help us now," Kimball grumbled. "So, December's supposed to be a good month to visit? Still seems like too many people to me."

"Rain keeps people away. And it's too cold for most campers. We'll basically have the place to ourselves," Jones said.

Kimball grunted. "Anyway, I'm bonked. We're ten miles from the Big Sur River Inn. That okay for a quick meal?" His passengers agreed but returned to sleeping and reading. Kimball didn't care. He had plenty to take in.

While the rest of the country lay in snow, December meant growth for most of California. At first, he thought the green cast to the ground was grass, but when he looked closer, he noticed the curling tips of ferns, an emerald mass spreading from the roadside up the hills. This delighted him. The tightness he had carried in his chest the past year loosened, and he felt himself surprised by his own joy. After everything that happened, he could still appreciate nature's beauty. She had not betrayed him.

The coast road headed inland. He followed it until the Inn's gravel lot appeared on his right. Since this wasn't tourist season, finding a parking spot was easy. His clients collected their things and followed Kimball. The Inn sat in an enclave consisting of the squat red building of the restaurant, the inn's guest rooms, a small store, and a multistory building of artists' studios, even a tavern.

"Must disappoint tourists who think they can drive into Big Sur and find cheap fast-food for the kids," Kimball said.

"Yeah, unfortunately," Smith said. "Development density is restricted to one unit per acre in tourist areas."

"What do you mean, unfortunately? Who the hell needs chains junking up the landscape?"

Smith shrugged.

"Most of the coastal region is owned by government or private agencies that don't allow any development," Jones added.

Miller continued the Wikipedia commentary, "The Big Sur Local Coastal Program, which preserves the region as open space, a small community, and ranching, was approved in 1981. It's extremely restrictive."

Kimball's lips pursed, his eyebrows drawing together. For people who barely glanced out their windows, they were damn knowledgeable about government regulations. His suspicions about the three being journalists were giving way to other ideas, but they were still his clients and responsibility. "Here we are, folks." He held the restaurant door open and forced a smile as they filed past him. Something was definitely up with the three.

After a lunch of burgers and steaks, they walked down to the Big Sur River with the three wandering off on their own. Kimball stood on the bank, appreciating the setting. A family occupied a couple of Adirondack chairs plunked down in shallow water. The husband was trying unsuccessfully to take a selfie of his large brood and Kimball offered to take the photo. Miller and Jones headed downstream. Kimball took the photo and handed the camera back to the dad.

From his peripheral vision, Kimball saw Miller take something from her pocket, crumple it, and toss it into the river. Kimball frowned. Had she just littered? A ball of white floated downstream. It might have been an accident. The two women were coming back his way. Kimball averted his eyes, focusing on the pine trees on the opposite shore. It had to be an accident.

"We should get going," Jones said. Kimball followed them up the path. Smith appeared, folding a pocketknife.

"We're going," Jones said to Smith.

The three walked ahead. Kimball noticed a tree sporting a blaze resembling the letter Z above two slashes, like some kind of branding on a cow's hide. Had Smith done that? This was something Kimball couldn't let go. He cleared his throat. "Hey, Smith."

The man turned to acknowledge Kimball. The women kept going.

"What's up with the knife?"

"Nothing. Just a knife. Why do you ask?" Smith's tone seemed to challenge Kimball, daring him to make an accusation. When he didn't answer, Smith continued to the car.

Kimball stared after the man. He wasn't sure if something was off with Smith or with himself. Kimball decided he was being sensitive. The accident probably caused him to swing too hard to the side of being overcautious. He thought of his initial conversation with Smith, who reassured Kimball he could do this trip—even though the newspapers had said those horrible things about him. Stop punishing yourself, Smith said. It had been an accident. Kimball reached the car and got behind the wheel. They continued southward. Maybe Smith was right. Kimball was too hard on himself.

"Hey, any of you want to stop at the bakery or the Henry Miller Library?" Kimball asked, trying to sound like a congenial tour guide. He glanced in the rearview mirror when no one answered him. The silence felt like a rebuke. "Okay, then we'll just check in at the ranger station," he said with a fake smile.

The map said Big Sur, but now Kimball understood the misconception he and others had, thinking Big Sur a town when it was more of a geographic region. A light concentration of buildings along a one-mile stretch of PCH delineated what people called Big Sur Village: vintage motor lodges, a general store, a post office, a couple of restaurants, a public library, plenty of artists' studios, and a smattering of other independent businesses. Concentration was a misnomer, since most of the buildings sat isolated, nestled amongst groves of pines and live oaks.

Kimball turned into the parking lot of the Big Sur Station, a multi-agency visitor center and ranger station operated by both the U.S. Forest Service and California State Parks. Before Kimball could ask if they wanted to accompany him, the three scurried off. Most of his clients wanted to tag along, meet the rangers, or buy souvenirs in the gift shop. He had to admit, he was more comfortable when the three weren't around.

Inside, a few tourists were taking in the educational nature exhibit. Kimball headed straight for the information counter.

"Hello. Checking in." He removed the passes from an envelope and set them on the counter.

"Kimball, right?" the ranger asked. "We've been expecting you." She picked up a pass and examined it. "Off-trail at this time of year?" She scowled. "You must have some pretty connected people with you to get these. This area you're going to has been closed to hikers since the last fires. This is Vicente Flat Camp." Her finger landed on the area map under a thick slab of glass. "Trailhead is here. That hike is nothing, child's play. This trail after the camp," her finger traced the dotted line, "even if you chose to stay on it, you'd still be alone at this time of year. Get the full experience."

He understood what she was getting at. Off-trail meant trudging through underbrush, scrambling over boulders and deadfall, and encountering who-knows-what. Couple all that with the impending rain and winter temperatures: everything would be wet and bone-chilling cold. "I've got clients with their hearts set on off-trail hiking in the middle of rainy season."

The ranger chuckled sardonically and shook her head. "Soggy boots and frigid nights make for miserable conditions. Forget bliss index," she said. "The misery index is going to be bad."

"Yeah, I told my clients it might be as low as 0, but this is what they want to do. I'm just the hired help."

She returned his passes. "Okay, Mr. Kimball, put this in your front window so you don't get towed away. And I don't need to give you the 'LNT' speech."

"Only footprints."

The ranger rapped the counter with both hands. "Well, you're all set, then. I've got you registered and expect you back here in three days. You be careful out there."

Kimball tried not to read too much into the warning. He nodded and thanked her.

A quick scan of the gift shop revealed his three clients weren't there. One more strange thing about them. On his way out, a painting near the door caught his attention. The subject drew him in—a forest cast in shadows, sun blocked out by redwoods, green foliage smudging the foreground—and something else. Kimball took a step closer. A black figure stood in the background amongst the tree trunks. When he studied the painting at an oblique angle, Kimball spotted another dark phantom, but when he looked directly at it, the shape disappeared into the forest.

"Benjamin Brode is the painter."

Kimball flinched, startled by the ranger's unexpected appearance beside him. "What are they?" he asked.

Lines creased the corners of the woman's mouth, replacing her earlier cheerful ranger-smile. "You see them, then?"

He pointed to the distinct figure. "And here." He gestured to the left side of the painting. "But I can't see this one head on."

"Local legend. The Spanish called them *Los Vigilantes Oscuros*. The Dark Watchers. The Chumash people used the term *nunasis*, benevolent and malevolent beings dwelling in the shadows of the forest. Wait." She went to the gift shop and returned with a book. "The artist teamed up with John Steinbeck's son for this project." Kimball flipped through the book of prints the ranger handed him. Not in each but in most, he caught glimpses of the shadowy phantoms. The ranger continued, "Some believe they protect the Santa Lucias."

Kimball nodded. He was familiar with this type of lore—beings that kept the forests safe from interlopers. From *Leshy* in the Slavic Regions to the *Kodama* of Japan, nature had to protect herself from man. "Have you seen them, the Dark Watchers?"

The ranger shook her head. "Want to, but it's never happened to me. How about you? All those trips to remote places over the years."

So she was familiar with him. He shook his head. "Me, neither. Felt things. That sacred presence that imbues all of nature." He didn't feel silly saying tree hugger crap to the ranger. "How come they're wearing tall hats and capes?"

"My theory is that the *nunasis*, the local spirits, took on the shape of the Spanish explorers because they perceived the newcomers as a threat. Hikers who come across them up here say they look like giants holding staffs. If you aren't harming nature, they leave you alone. Or it could just be the Brocken spectre phenomenon," the ranger said, referring to the optical illusion.

Kimball handed the book back to the ranger. "I don't care if it's ghosts or someone just seeing their shadow. Whatever spooky story it takes to keep people from fucking up nature is fine by me." He stuck his hand out and the ranger shook it. "Thanks for everything."

He glanced over his shoulder as he left. She was still standing there, book in hand, staring after him with a worried look.

Back at the Suburban, Kimball's clients were nowhere in sight. He didn't want to think about what they might be doing. In the back seat, one of their bags was unzipped and a book peeked out. Kimball glanced around. He wanted to have his suspicions allayed and he felt justified in snooping. Either something was going on with the three, or he was losing it. He opened the door and slipped the book from the bag. The cover was leather, symbols carved into the material. He opened it. The odor of old combined with something sour wafted up his nostrils, making him sneeze. Same awful stink he'd been smelling all day, but worse. He heard the crunch of leaves behind him and his head whipped around. Just a squirrel rifling about for acorns. He returned his attention to the book. The sepia-colored pages were thick but not brittle, as would be expected from something that seemed ancient, but he surmised the pages were vellum, prepared animal skin. The exterior symbols were repeated inside. As he leafed through, a page with slash marks stood out. He thought of the blaze on the tree at the inn. *Who the hell are these people?*

The crunch of gravel and animated voices alerted Kimball. He looked up and saw the three heading for the car. He tried to shove the book into the bag, but it tumbled to the floor. Kimball scowled at the wayward book, trying to decide whether to right it or leave it. The first rain drops pattered onto the roof. Kimball reached for the book. The three picked up their pace. At the last minute, he abandoned the book and eased the door shut.

"We're all set," Kimball said a little too cheerfully as he got behind the wheel. The rain arrived in a thunderous avalanche.

The three scrambled into the SUV without speaking to him. As he backed out of the space, Kimball heard the backpack being zippered closed.

"The turn off isn't far," Jones said. "A left after we pass Limekiln State Park."

"Just imagine it," Miller said. "Late 1800s, the lime from here was used to make cement for places like San Francisco. Had all the resources right here to do it: limestone and plenty of wood from those massive trees, which were much bigger then and more plentiful, perfect for the kilns. They even rigged up a cable line right down to the cove at the shore to get the barrels to the ships quickly. Genius."

"Sure, but," Kimball said, "they decimated the forest in a few short years."

"Yeah, put them out of business. Men lost their jobs," Smith said.

Kimball heard their tone and realized he and the three weren't having the same conversation. The lime kilns sounded interesting, though, as an artifact. He decided to make a stop after he took the three on their excursion.

The rain was coming down in hard drops, sounding like marbles plunking on the roof of the vehicle. He had to keep an eye out for the left turn.

The sign at the entrance to the Nacimiento-Fergusson Road stated "Closed to through traffic." Kimball drove around it. The road was the only one in the middle of the state connecting the California coast to California inland. Besides campgrounds and trails, Fort Hunter-Liggett, an Army installation, was situated on the east end of the road. It was also the fastest and easiest way to access the heart of the Santa Lucias, but the sign at the entrance and the road's reputation for being perilous kept most people out.

The road spiraled upward, creating the illusion it was winding into the sky. Here the world divided: on his left a rugged rock wall and to the right the Pacific Ocean. The clouds parted for a moment; ocean and sky melded into one expanse of blue. "Wow, look at that view." Kimball's reaction was spontaneous. Over the course of his career as a guide, nature's beauty still overwhelmed him, as if his mind couldn't retain images of such awesomeness and had to be constantly reminded. Maybe that was nature's trick. If people became blasé about mountains and oceans and sunrises, then nature was doomed to mankind's two diseases—greed and relentless progress.

Only one car could take the corkscrew curves at a time. As they climbed in elevation, coastal scrub gave way to fir trees. On the last curve, they reached cloud level. A ghost mist floated amongst the trees. Though it was still early afternoon, a murky gloom muddied time. Kimball glanced at the clock to make sure they hadn't suddenly lost hours. No, it was just past 3 p.m.

The mist forced him to drive cautiously around the bends, watching for oncoming cars. Kimball drove around a pile of rocks that had slid from the mountainside. Lights approached. Kimball slowed and moved to the far right, tires riding the edge of road and sky. Once safely past the oncoming car, he resumed the middle of the road. It would be the last car they came across.

Kimball drove in silence, thinking about everything he had encountered that day: the books, the arcane marks, the weird behavior of the three. They didn't speak like his other clients, who were nature-focused. The three's conversations favored business and money. Kimball's suspicions now pointed toward developers or, something worse, environmental terrorists who scoped out ways to end or curb protections on untouched lands. He had encountered these types a few times in his career. He glanced at his rearview mirror and decided that neither Smith nor Miller looked like any type of terrorists. Scholars, more like. Jones did fit the Mata Hari type, though. Nothing made sense.

Kimball noticed something up ahead. A figure, just off the road, stood amongst the trees. Hiking was restricted and the small campgrounds in the area closed because of the last round of fires. As the Suburban rushed toward the spot, Kimball made out the outline of a cape and tall hat. The painting from the station flashed through his mind. This wasn't a hiker. Beads of sweat rose to the surface of his skin. The sensation was familiar, like the morning of the accident. He wanted to vomit his own internal organs. The figure grew taller. Instead of becoming more distinct, its blackness grew denser, as if swallowing the surrounding shadows. Fear and anxiety mixed a cocktail in his bloodstream, urging him to turn around, go back. Instead, Kimball pressed down on the gas pedal and his heart kept pace. His eyes focused on a spot a mile ahead on the road.

"What's going on?" Jones asked.

Kimball glanced at her. The dark figure materialized at her window. It was as clear as if he had pulled over to have a look. Kimball grabbed Jones, pulling her toward him, away from the window, and it. His panic dissipated as soon as they passed the spot where the phantom had stood. He released his grip on Jones's arm. He couldn't remember why he had been so frightened—just shadows in the mist playing tricks on him.

"Hey, what happened?" Miller asked.

"Nothing."

"Did you see something?" Smith asked.

Tell them no. Admit nothing. "Just a deer too close to the edge of the road." He felt Jones staring at him, the other two hovering at his shoulder. "I thought we were going to hit it."

Jones watched him with her blue eyes, as if waiting for him to split open, truth spilling out of him like a sticky syrup she could lap up. After a minute staring at him, she turned her attention back to the map. "The Forest Road is up ahead."

"Too bad you didn't hit it," Miller said. "Would have made an excellent dinner."

"Seriously?" Kimball looked at her in the rearview mirror. "Hitting a deer with a car is never a good thing—not for the deer or us."

Miller shrugged and went back to her books.

Kimball shivered, a combination of disgust and a vague creeping fear. He couldn't wait for this trip to end. The Forest Road appeared and he turned left onto it. In the growing darkness, the trees seemed to hug the sides of the road, squeezing the passage into a narrow channel. Kimball watched the shadows. His passengers put away their distractions and moved closer to their own windows. They craned their necks, watching the forest as closely as he was.

After twenty miles of what primarily consisted of switchbacks, they arrived at the Vincente Flat Trailhead. Kimball pulled into one of the parking spaces. His was the only vehicle. He set the brake and was about to review the route and lay out the rules when the three bailed from the back seat before he said go. He slammed his door and marched around to the back of the Suburban. His nostrils quivered and his ears burned scarlet. His stance was wide legged, hands on his hips. The three were pulling on rain ponchos, but Kimball's was still in his pack. Rain dripped down his head, like eggs being dropped on him from above. He wiped his face and tried to act stern.

"Look, I don't know what's up with you guys. You obviously don't need me to lead you. You seem to have your own plans that I don't know about. So what the hell am I doing here?"

Three faces turned to him, hoods drawn over their heads, making them appear like high priests considering a lowly cleric. The rain beat a rhythm, like warning drums on the tree leaves, the Suburban's roof, the ground.

"We needed a guide, Kimball." Smith's words were measured and careful as if he were speaking to someone about to come unhinged. "You're our guide. You're one of the world's best. The accident was going to take that away from you. We thought we'd give you your second chance."

Kimball sucked his lips in and looked from Smith to Miller to Jones. They, standing before him in their matching rain gear, waited for Kimball to say something. His water drenched clothing felt heavy, his penance for ridiculous behavior. Maybe he was exaggerating the situation. Those red flags he saw all day—maybe those were just his own insecurities waving about in his head. The problem wasn't the three. The problem was him. "Sorry. Guess I'm still a little touchy."

"No problem," Smith said.

"We should get going," Jones suggested.

"Don't want this to be a nero day," Miller added.

Vicente Flat Camp lay two miles from the trailhead. They would get dry and have a good night's sleep for the much longer trek the next day. Kimball watched for shadowy figures, but the short hike was uneventful. The rain even abated. The camp consisted of a clearing and a firepit made of stacked stone, surrounded by logs serving as seats. Kimball assigned jobs and, much to his relief, everyone took to their tasks without complaint. The tents went up first.

Jones took out a hatchet. "I'm going to try to find some dry kindling and wood." Miller accompanied her.

After they built the fire, Smith started supper. Kimball's unease melted away as the group worked together. After they had eaten, they drank herbal tea and watched the flames—normal camp behavior. The day had been long and tiresome. The crackle of the fire soothed him. Kimball closed his eyes.

When he opened them again, he found hiker midnight had come and gone. Only Smith sat on the other side of the firepit. The women had gone off together to tend to personal matters. Kimball decided to do likewise. He grabbed his spade and his water bottle bidet. Even though he tried to head in the opposite direction he thought Miller and Jones had gone, he heard the women talking. He changed course and found a secluded spot to dig his cat hole.

Chanting drifted his way, followed by a piercing shriek. He curtailed his ablutions and chased after the cry. He crept forward, fallen leaves mush beneath his feet. Voices came from behind an outcropping of boulders. He squeezed through an opening in the rocks. As he worked his way deeper, the boulders arched over him, forming a shelter. Jones and Miller stood before a rock wall with Miller holding a flashlight as she chanted in a guttural language Kimball didn't recognize. Jones held a can of spray paint, slashes of red on the walls. White handprints were being obliterated. Kimball remembered seeing pictures of them in his research of the area.

He erupted. "Hey, goddamn it!"

The flashlight turned in his direction, blinding him.

"You can't do that!" he yelled. "What the fuck? Those are ancient Esselen handprints. Get out of here."

A light rushed toward him. Kimball backpedaled in defense, stepped on a rock and fell hard on his right side. The flashlight beam swept past him. Kimball rolled to his feet and went after the women. A gust of wind pressed at his back, forcing Kimball to stop and hold up his spade, expecting Smith behind him. He turned to face the man, but saw black shadows melting into the night. He waited for movement, a snap of a branch, the detectable breath of a person watching him. When there was nothing, he dashed back to camp to find the three sitting casually around the firepit. Kimball toed the boundary between the darkness and firelight, too angry to approach.

"I've had enough," he spat. "I believed your little story back there at the car, but you've been gaslighting me all day. And after what I just saw, what I've seen all day, I want to know what's going on." He clenched his fists and threw his shoulders back. Again, they stared indifferently at him. "Fine. We're leaving now. I have to report the vandalism to the ranger. Jesus Christ."

"Look around, Mr. Kimball," Smith said, menace icing his voice. "It's night, too dark to walk miles back to the car. Don't you think?"

"The trail is right there. Two miles is nothing," Kimball said.

Miller gave him a flat look. "I'm too frightened," she whimpered. "I'll need to stay here for the night." Her voice and posture contradicted one another.

"I'm scared, too," Jones giggled. "I'm not walking back at this time of night. What if a bear eats me?"

"Well, I'm leaving," Kimball said.

"So you would abandon us here? We can't find our way back in the dark." Smith's voice sounded like a wounded animal but his face registered dispassion. "What would people say?"

"He can't seem to take care of his clients," Jones mocked. "Leaves them to die."

Heat shot up from Kimball's gut to his face. Here they were at last—the real Smith, Miller, and Jones. These three had come to destroy and he was their scapegoat. Kimball was the incompetent guide, the one with blood on his hands, and they innocent clients. That would be the story they told, because after the accident, his word meant nothing.

He threw the spade at them and ran for the trail. Jones cut him off and flipped him over her back. Kimball and the ground collided. Jones came down hard, digging a knee into his solar plexus, holding him in place. Smith and Miller came over. Black pit eyes and mouth slashes looked down at him. The distortion caused by the firelight and his perspective made Kimball see demons, not humans.

"You're not working out for us," Smith said. "All you had to do was be our guide, and you can't even fill that role. I suggest you crawl into your tent and stay there for the rest of the night."

"The fuck I will." Kimball struggled against Jones, who pressed harder.

Smith picked up the hatchet, smacking the flat side of the head against his palm. "Get inside your tent." Jones took her weight off Kimball, who rolled to his feet. "I'm a good aim with this. Do you want to try me?"

"Okay, I'm going." His knife and cell phone were in the tent.

Miller held up those two objects and then threw both into the dark. Smith herded Kimball into his tent. Jones yanked the zippers closed, padlocking the sliders together.

"Just stay there, Mr. Kimball," Smith said. "Ladies, looks as if we need to attend to business tonight."

They snuffed out the fire. Darkness descended over the tent. Unable to see, Kimball strained to listen. Over his pounding heart, he heard their footsteps moving away from the camp. When he was sure they were gone, he groped around the tent for something to defend himself. His clothes and sleeping bag were missing. God, how could he be so fucking stupid?

He squatted on the tent floor; cold seeping up from the ground stung his buttocks. They had taken everything just to make him uncomfortable. He drew his knees up and rested his forehead against them. Shit, all the weird stuff he chose to overlook or excuse. He had accepted the job because he needed the money, but he also wanted to prove he could return to the field. He just wanted his old life back, to have a purpose in this world, and not be thought of as a loser, a has-been. He rocked back and forth to warm himself. Something jabbed his thigh. When he dug into his pocket, he found his car keys.

Footsteps approached his tent.

"Who's there?" Kimball held still. "I'm not afraid of you."

The tent shook.

"Let me out of here."

Someone was walking the perimeter of the tent. Then one side ripped open. A dark figure stood in silhouette against the night sky. Kimball saw the outline of the tall hat and the drape of a cloak—the same phantom he observed earlier.

Several more emerged out of the dark. Terror seized up Kimball's muscles and he couldn't move. His mind was playing tricks on him. They couldn't be the phantoms from the painting he had seen at the station. The Dark Watchers, like all the other nature spirits, were myths.

One of them lifted an arm and pointed to the forest. The figures melted into the darkness.

The terror subsided. Kimball crawled from the tent, keys digging into his palm. The car wasn't far.

A scream, human in its pain, strengthened Kimball's resolve to escape. He should run.

Another scream sliced through the night. "Fuck." He shoved the keys back into his pocket and set off into the forest, toward the screaming.

Dark figures materialized, running alongside him. One brushed up against him. Kimball's arm burned as if acid ate through his skin. This was not a dream or a case of pareidolia. He shied away from the phantoms, but they stayed beside him, their cloaks streaming in the wind.

He looked forward, avoiding side glances at the apparitions. An orange glow and chanting steered him toward a clearing. Kimball hid behind a tree, wanting to size up the situation before he rushed in. The phantoms remained with him.

A bear hung from the tree, rear legs bound, nose down. It thrashed about like a hooked fish. With the hatchet, Smith slashed the bear's hide. The animal roared, whipping a paw tipped with daggers at its torturer. Smith ducked and retreated.

Kimball fell to his knees and covered his mouth to stifle his own scream. Three small fires formed a triangle, with the bear dangling at its center. Miller was reading from one of the musty tomes as Jones gyrated and shook, dancing around the fires and the bear.

A Dark Watcher materialized at the center of the fire triangle, summoned by the bear's pain. The chanting grew louder and more forceful; Jones writhed and cavorted faster. The Watcher tried reaching for the bear, but the phantom's arms were pinned to its sides, trapped by a spell of words and arcane rituals. Smith chopped at the bear's flesh. The Watcher shuddered. The faster Jones danced and Miller chanted, the faster the trapped phantom vibrated, becoming a blur. The three stepped back from the fires. The Dark Watcher exploded, sparks shooting skyward.

Smith sprinted back to the bear and cut it once again. The hatchet's blade dripped black. Another dark figure appeared within the fire triangle and the process resumed until that Dark Watcher was destroyed as well.

A Watcher touched Kimball's back. He winced but faced the entity. The Watcher possessed no features, but as Kimball gazed into a pool of inky blackness, he knew what it wanted. Kimball shuddered. The keys were still in his pocket. The Watcher grabbed Kimball's forearm, the entity's hand like the stinger of a wasp. Yes, he understood that this was his fault. He brought the three to this place. Running away was not an option. Another Watcher pushed him into the open. They were right. He had to do something before they killed more Watchers.

"Hey, over here!" Kimball yelled, waving his arms.

Miller faced him and directed the chanting at him, throwing out a hand in his direction. Kimball's head whipped back as if hit with a hammer. He righted himself and charged Miller. With a wave of her hand, she flung Kimball aside. He tried to rationalize what had just happened, but it became clear to him. He now knew what kind of environmental terrorists he was dealing with.

He put his head down and rammed Miller, knocking her breath from her. With the chanting disrupted, the trapped Dark Watcher stepped out of the prison created by the triangle of fires. Miller turned her attention back to it. Kimball rushed her again, knocking the woman into the Watcher. It swallowed Miller up in the folds of its cloak. When they fell open, she was gone.

Jones howled, leaping onto Kimball's back. Smith, hatchet held above his head, rushed Kimball. He couldn't fight them both. He shook off Jones and ran. The Suburban was too far. He remembered from maps that Limekiln Park was below him and then the highway. Kimball ran westward. He plunged down the side of the mountain, hoping the fall line didn't have any surprises like a cliff. When the pitch became too steep, he crabbed his way down, digging his boots into the hillside as he struggled for traction.

From above, he heard Smith and Jones crashing through the brush, coming for him. Kimball stumbled, felt himself free-falling. A Watcher appeared, righting him. Its touch burned his flesh, but he was relieved to have his feet planted firmly on the earth.

Jones screamed. Kimball crouched, expecting an attack. Instead, she careened past him. Her momentum down the steep hill was too great and she flew into a tree, spine snapping like a tree branch. Smith couldn't be far. Kimball scrambled on.

A line of Watchers appeared, startling him, and he slid to a stop, his boots touching the hems of their capes. Behind the Watchers, four dark giants loomed against the night sky, the ruins of the lime kilns. The Watchers disappeared, revealing the edge of a cliff. They had saved him.

Kimball stayed low and scooted to his left until he found a path. Cramps felt like dagger jabs in his sides. He had to stop. The effects of drinking daily for months had impaired his abilities. Even if Smith was nearby, Kimball needed to rest for just a few minutes. The Watchers encircled him and guided him to one of the kilns, pushing him into an opening whose jagged and broken bricks looked like a mouth filled with fangs waiting to swallow him whole. Every time the Watchers touched him, Kimball wanted to howl with pain.

The woods snapped and rustled. Kimball curled up inside the kiln.

"Where are you, Kimball?" Smith yelled. "Let's talk."

Kimball massaged his sides and tried to relax. He had to be ready to flee.

"The world's changing, Kimball. Humans rule it. Not Mother Nature or dead ancestors or forest spirits. Humans have a right to this world. We have to let the old gods know that it's our time."

Smith was wrong. Kimball had spent his whole life amongst the mountains and forests. He thought of the mornings he lay awake in his warm sleeping bag under a naked sky, the morning air biting, dew on everything, and having that first cup of hot coffee fresh out of a pot bubbling on the grate of a fire, a hawk circling above his head. The forest was his temple, the mountains his spiritual guide. Now Smith was telling him those things no longer mattered. Kimball had led Her disciples. They followed him onto mountain peaks and across vast prairies. They witnessed fish leaping into the air as if they were trying to join the birds winging across the skies, and birds plummeting into watery depths, staying submerged for so long Kimball thought they had turned into fish themselves. Humans finding the numinous in nature mattered. When it stopped mattering, then humanity would be damned. And here in these California mountains, the Dark Watchers stood strong for hundreds of years against the encroachment of humans. He would stand up for nature anytime. Kimball crawled out of the kiln, ready to fight.

A club came down across Kimball's back, sending him sprawling to the ground. Smith raised the club to smash Kimball's skull. Kimball rolled over and kicked Smith's right knee, snapping it out of alignment, kneecap twisted to the left. Smith howled and flopped backward onto the ground. Kimball got up and stood over Smith.

An incantation erupted from Smith's mouth, sending Kimball flying. Like some slithering monster, Smith crawled toward Kimball. Each foreign word Smith uttered felt like a noose. Kimball clawed at his neck, but the invisible restraint became tighter and tighter until his vision blurred at the edges. Smith was killing him.

Kimball booted Smith in the mouth. Free from Smith's spell, Kimball struggled to his feet.

He made it to the Pacific Coast Highway, where he collapsed. His skin burned. Black spots pocked his skin. He watched the tree line for Smith. He called out to the Dark Watchers. No one came. His body and mind rebelled against all he had witnessed that night, finally shutting down and leaving him stranded on the side of the road.

A passerby found him curled up on the side of the PCH, bruised and unresponsive. The Good Samaritan's phone managed one bar of reception, enough to reach 911. A car from the Monterey Sheriff's Office arrived first, followed soon after by an EMS rig. When the deputy approached him, Kimball came out of his blackout, screaming for them not to touch him. He lurched about in the breakdown lane as the first responders tried to keep him from stumbling into oncoming traffic. The deputy coaxed

Kimball into sitting on the bumper of the ambulance and then lying on the gurney.

In the back of the antiseptically clean ambulance, Kimball's mind began to doubt what he had experienced. Screaming bears, shadows in capes, magical incantations. He said two words aloud, "Dark Watchers," and they carried no weight under those bright electric lights.

"What did you say?" the paramedic asked.

Kimball couldn't remember. "What?"

The woman shrugged. Out of habit, she reached for his wrist to take his vitals.

Kimball flinched. "Don't touch me."

"Okay, I won't. You're safe here." She picked up a clipboard and pen. "Can you tell me your name?"

He blinked several times. He was sure he still had a name. She started to write.

"Harris Kimball."

The paramedic glanced up, then smiled in encouragement. "Great."

The deputy and the second paramedic opened the doors of the ambulance. As they discussed Kimball, he looked beyond them, into the darkness. And he remembered. "Dark Watchers."

The paramedic jerked away, color draining from her face.

"You okay?" the deputy asked.

"Did you just hear what he said?"

The deputy and second paramedic shook their heads.

The paramedic understood. Kimball repeated the words.

"He keeps repeating *Dark Watchers*." The words sounded like dry leaves in her mouth, the letters brittle between tongue and palate.

Kimball bolted upright like a jack-in-the-box, catching the paramedics and deputy off guard. With panic-glazed eyes, he stared past them into the night. "Dark Watchers," Kimball said loudly. "I saw them."

"Hey, lie back." The paramedic pressed his shoulder.

Kimball recoiled. "Don't touch me. Don't touch me. Don't touch me." He pushed up his shirt sleeves. Black splotches creeped up his forearms.

"Those look like handprints," the deputy said.

Kimball watched as the dark ichor spread, consuming his body. The paramedics and deputy backed away. He understood now, his purpose clear. Smith was still out there, and so many others like him. Kimball staggered out of the ambulance. The darkness beckoned him.

He pulled his cloak around him and walked into the forest. The Dark Watchers, his brothers, were waiting for him.

## ABOUT THE AUTHOR

E.S. Magill loves writing and anything horror or supernatural. Combining her two loves, she became a dark fiction writer and has had short stories published in anthologies such as *California Screamin'* and *Blood Lite III*. In addition to writing, she edited two anthologies, *Haunted Mansion Project: Year One* and *Deep Cuts* (co-edited with Angel Leigh McCoy and Chris Marrs). She served as the Reviews Editor for *Dark Wisdom* magazine, where she also wrote the column "The Dark Librarian." She holds a B.A. and M.A. in English, specializing in the postmodern gothic. Recently retired from teaching middle school English, she now spends her days writing, reading, binge-watching all things horror. Her love of the craft prompted her to start a small publishing company creating nonfiction workbooks for writers, www.scribesandscribblerspub.com. She considers herself a lifelong Californian but recently moved to Phoenix along with her also-retired husband Greg. Look for her new supernatural series coming Summer 2022. Visit www.esmagill.com to sign up for E.S. Magill's newsletter "The Dark Write of the Soul."

# Recall

Yvonne Navarro

Three a.m.:

Warren Hastings was getting ready to take a shower and the cheap Bluetooth speaker in his cramped bathroom was playing "Eli's Coming." At the start of the organ wail that signaled the end of the song, static cut through the music and climbed to the whine of a dispatcher's words as he rattled off an address in a bored voice. The choppy sound of the police band was such a familiar one to Warren's ears that it didn't even register until he heard the word *Glenwood* and the radio abruptly returned to Three Dog Night singing *"Whoa-oo, whoa-oo."*

His hand stopped reaching for the shower curtain and he blinked at the speaker on the windowsill. What was that? *Glenwood*, the dispatcher had said. No...he must have imagined it. A freak spreading of sound waves, that's all; the little speaker might be cheap, but it had a good wireless connection and was picking up calls from the local cop shop. He'd just moved into this small rental house yesterday and had finished unpacking tonight; the window had seemed like a good place for the speaker, but the glass was surrounded by a metal frame. If there was going to be a problem with interference—

He heard the sudden, sharp sound of his cell phone ringing in the living room.

Warren frowned and stepped out of the bathroom, not bothering to wrap a towel around himself or grab a robe to cover his naked body; there was no one else to see him, anyway. Who the hell would call him at this time of night? Sure, he had a buddy or two who might still be up, but even if those guys weren't already winding down, they had better things to do than call him. He picked it up and swiped Accept.

"Hello?" He let the tone of his voice make it obvious to the caller that he was more than a little annoyed.

*"Warren, it's me,"* his mother's trembling voice whispered. *"You have to come quickly—I think someone's trying to break into the basement! Your father can't—"*

He hit the disconnect button and dropped the phone.

Then sat on the couch in a cold sweat until dawn.

He slept until 1:30, then rose and took the shower he'd forgotten about the previous night. The hot water helped beat some sense back into him; the call now seemed like little more than a bad dream. The past year had been the sort of wide-awake nightmare that he used to believe happened only to others, or maybe to the crime victims he saw nearly every day. Add the recent move and working himself to exhaustion over finagling a way to live in this small suburb west of Chicago... It was a miracle he hadn't outright cracked.

Moist steam billowed around him and he breathed deeply, almost smiling at the realization that he was sort of an illegal immigrant out here, since as a Chicago cop and city employee, he was supposed to live within the city limits. His ass would really be on the line if he were caught, but the city's ultimate act of violence had finally driven him out, turned him into the suburbanite he'd always disdained. His personnel file now read that he lived with his older brother, Clark, in a new townhouse development not far from the district where Warren had been reassigned. Only a few close friends knew his new cell number.

Warren killed the day and kept his mind occupied by doing all the things he'd never had to worry about in his years as an apartment dweller: mowing the grass, gathering dead branches and yard debris, a hundred other little chores that, while he hadn't counted on them, at least acted as a balm for the sore place the telephone call—which he'd finally decided was a nasty prank his tired brain had imagined into something else—had left on his mind. When most of his neighbors were sitting down to dinner at six o'clock, Warren was still working in the yard; pulling second shift for the last ten years had permanently ingrained upon his body the habit that dinner was not until at least eight, bedtime never earlier than two in the morning.

When it got too dark for him to see what he was doing, Warren went inside without much hope and checked the fridge for something to eat. There was a frozen turkey dinner, but he didn't have a microwave, so he decided it would be easier to simply wash his face and hands, then jump in the car. There was a Chinese take-out place not far from the house; he could phone in the order and pick it up in fifteen minutes.

He switched on the Bluetooth speaker and looked at his reflection in the mirror above the sink as he listened to the oldies from his phone. Warren could see his father in the lines of his own face, especially in the almost colorless gray eyes beneath the short, unevenly cut sandy hair. He tried to think of the man as he had once been, before the bullet fired by a still-unapprehended stranger had made a hole in his father's spine that never quite healed, before the hospital beds and diapers. But the early memories brought pain: his father had been a violent man who had seen his years on the police force as little more than a tool of power for which he drew a paycheck. Had the elder Hastings not been disabled when Warren was barely into his teens, he might have followed the same mental track into a life of viciousness and intimidation. As it was, Warren Hastings was one of the few cops in his precinct who really believed force should be a last resort.

Incomprehensible static bled through the speaker for a few seconds, garbling the announcer's voice and making it seem like two or three people were trying to broadcast at once. The transmission faded as quickly as it had come and, before Warren could blink, the disc jockey rolled into Supertramp's "The Logical Song."

Nerves jangling, he grabbed a jacket and left the house. He sat in his car and tried to calm himself before pulling out of the driveway, especially when he realized his knuckles had paled where they curled around the steering wheel. His appetite was gone. When he nosed the heavy old Buick up to the intersection at Irving Park Road, he decided to turn east and simply drive for a while, let the feel of the tires and the smooth motion of the car rolling along the highway soothe him. As a kid, in the years before his father's accident, he'd dreamed not of becoming a cop like his old man, but a truck driver, sitting high above the traffic in the cab of an eighteen-wheeler. He wondered now if that childish wish hadn't really been a subconscious desire to escape.

In the early June drizzle, he concentrated more on the actual motions of driving than on direction, keeping an eye on the traffic-laden streets sporting the usual hordes of Saturday night couples and teenagers, sober and otherwise. The expressway unwound beneath the car like a long, wet snake and Warren felt himself gradually relaxing, the blood that had been thudding in his temples slowing. His vision, which had been on the verge of twitching, finally steadied.

He was more resigned than surprised when he turned onto Glenwood, though he was already railing silently at himself for coming. Still, he pulled into an obscenely convenient parking space across from his parents' old house and studied the small structure. Who lived there now? Perhaps a younger family, with a couple of kids to go in the long-empty bedrooms, or another retired couple like his Mom and Dad. And had they fixed that basement window yet? The little house was dark and draped in shadows, with no side spotlights and the nearest streetlight at least thirty feet away. The gangway that ran along the left side was nothing but a deep, black slash filled with possibilities.

Warren stayed there, just watching, until hunger forced him to start the car and find a greasy hamburger joint. As he chewed and swallowed the last of the rubbery meat and watched a couple of punk kids playing a video game in the corner, he suddenly wondered what he was doing, back here in the city that he so detested, blowing a Saturday night by hanging around a house that had been sold three seasons ago. How stupid to be doing this, dragging things out, reliving feelings that should have been put to rest at the very latest with the sale of the house. He dumped the rest of his oil-drenched crinkle fries in the trash and went home.

The dispatcher's voice, escalating to a sudden, startling snarl, woke Warren from the doze he'd slipped into, snapping his senses into sharpness with the instinctive skill of a veteran cop.

—*burglary in progress, proceed code two, five-six-two-four Glenwood. Time out, fifteen oh-eight.*

The static-filled voice faded into the soft mumblings of a song Warren couldn't identify. He could see into the bathroom from where he'd been dozing in the circular softness of the decades-old papasan chair in front of the television; backgrounded by the heavy glass blocks, the Bluetooth speaker crouched on the windowsill like an evil, black plastic gargoyle sent to destroy the peacefulness of his new home. The moment of panic lengthened, until Warren realized he'd simply forgotten to turn it off after his earlier shower.

*5624 Glenwood.*

Jesus.

His cell phone rang and Warren moaned, but was still unable to stop from answering it. He opened his mouth but no words could move past the clot of fear in his throat.

*"Warren?"* His mother's voice, so sweet to his ears even through her terror.

"Yes." It was more of a sigh than an actual word.

*"Warren, I think someone's trying to break in one of the basement windows. I've already called 911. Can you come?"*

"Mom," he said miserably, "I c-can't. I've moved—I won't be able to make it...in time." He was cold, so cold, in fact, that his rigid legs were moving independently of his will, shivering and nearly knocking his knees against each other. His stomach twisted in sick fright, his heart laboring. Silence then, stretching and stretching and stretching as he watched the display on the DVD player flip to 3:09 a.m. "Mom?"

Then, *"It's okay, son. I understand."*

Forgiveness.

And a dial tone.

Fingers shaking badly, he dialed Clark's number.

"Hello?" His older brother's voice dripped with sleep. Warren felt a sudden, fierce jealousy of that ability—how he'd like to be able to rest, sink into numbed oblivion, as easily as his sibling.

"Clark," he said. "Mom just called." Warren's voice was thick and hoarse, as though his throat and vocal chords were wrapped in heavy sandpaper. Part of him couldn't believe he was actually saying those words; another took a snide and bitter pleasure in destroying his brother's slumber for the rest of the night. And this would do it, yes sir.

"Warren," Clark said sharply—and wasn't it amazing how he suddenly sounded so awake? "Oh, man...." Warren could tell Clark was struggling to bring his tone under control, make it softer and not so critical, more diplomatic. His brother's deep breath was like a whistling through the telephone line, and the sound of it, this symbol of impatience, flooded Warren with resentment.

"This is just too sad, you know?" Clark said carefully. "Let it *go*, buddy. You couldn't have made any difference, okay?"

"But—"

"But nothing," Clark interrupted. "It's been almost a year." The other man hesitated and Warren found himself staring at the DVD player again: 3:11. Something inside him did a slow, agonized flip. He heard Clark's words and realized he didn't know what his brother had been saying.

"What?" Warren asked blankly. "What did you say?"

"I said maybe you should go, you know, talk to somebody. Don't they have staff psychologists or social workers or something like that in the department?"

"I already did that. The captain required it."

"So *go back*," Clark said. "Man, you should be *over* this by now."

"*Over* it?" Warren asked. The thought was incredible.

"You know what I'm saying," Clark snapped. "Don't twist shitty meanings into my words."

"I-I'm sorry," Warren said slowly. "You're right. Maybe I *should* talk to someone again."

"That's my boy." His brother seemed relieved. "You can get through this, okay? I have great faith in you, kid. Now get some sleep."

"Sure," Warren agreed. "G'night."

As he hung up the telephone, his eyes found the DVD player again. 3:13.

*Sleep.*

What a laugh.

Warren wanted very badly to drive past his parents' house again, do it in the squad car at the very start of his shift, when the late afternoon sun was shining and the temperature had climbed to the point where it gave everything that sense of clarity that only a perfect, early summer day can have. That, of course, was impossible; he had been reassigned eleven months ago and it was no longer his district. He could do it anyway and risk a four hundred dollar fine if one of the beat sergeants spotted him, but his partner, Mitch, a drawn-faced second-year kid who still did everything by the book, would never go for it. Warren wouldn't have been able to explain the need to Mitch anyway; they weren't close like the coppers you always saw on the television shows. Even though he and the kid hadn't exactly clicked—not yet, anyway—Warren thought that he and Mitch could have a good friendship going in a few years, once the younger man got his head out of the do-gooder clouds and returned to real life. Maybe that's why, when the two of them called in for down time and went into an Italian place called Colleti's on Higgins and Austin for dinner, he decided to tell Mitch what had happened.

"You're quiet tonight," Mitch commented when they settled into a booth. He didn't say anything else, just waited with his hands folded in front of him like a schoolboy. Warren had to appreciate his partner's patience; he knew the rumors had flown around the station back when he'd first been transferred. Mitch had been a rookie then, eager to get involved in everything and still believing in *Miami Vice* partnerships between squadmates. Despite his enthusiasm, Mitch had never questioned Warren about the stories, as if he'd known there was a time to talk and a time to mind your own business.

Tonight was Warren's time to talk.

The waitress came and he ordered something by reflex—spaghetti, ravioli, something, it didn't matter. She had barely stepped away when he opened his mouth and the words spilled out like the rejected remains of a spoiled plate of food.

"My parents were murdered a year ago tonight."

Mitch didn't say anything; Warren could see in the kid's eyes that he probably already knew the story but was willing to hear it firsthand. Still, the unexpected anniversary caused a little ripple in Mitch's stony facade.

"It was a home invasion, in the same district where I was working, too. In fact, I was only a few blocks away, but I didn't even know it was going down." Warren's hands found the linen napkin and began working at the fabric. "George—that's my old partner—and I had answered a disturbance call on Berwyn, somebody throwing a party and the music was too loud, that kind of bullshit. The guy was drunk and hollering. With the music and all, our radios were just more noise adding to the parade. Couldn't even hear the dispatcher." Warren could still remember the call: the two of them, standing in the foyer of an apartment building that looked nice on the outside but was starting to show decay in the worn carpet beneath their feet and the spider-thin cracks climbing the paint-encrusted walls. And the guy in the apartment, a half-soused millennial explaining to the dumb little policemen that the music couldn't possibly be too loud, it didn't even begin to get loud, see, until the volume dial was turned to *four*, and he only had it set on *three*, understand?

Warren worked on the napkin some more, straining to keep his voice from sounding ragged. "There I was, less than a half mile away, while three teenage psychopaths busted in a basement window of my Mom and Dad's house." He clenched his teeth for a moment, concentrating on the feeling of the muscles working in his jaw to keep his eyes from filling with the familiar tears. "The hell of it was we did a drive-by after the call had gone through dispatch and a squad was on its way, only I didn't know anything was wrong."

"How did you find out?" Mitch asked quietly. The younger man's face was pinched and unhappy, the skin pale and shining in the darkened restaurant. Despite Mitch's question, Warren never got the impression his partner didn't want to hear the rest of it.

"George and I were just cruising, you know, when I heard a guy call in for a homicide set-up and a meat wagon to my parents' address at twenty minutes after three. I shouldn't have gone over there, but I *had* to—I mean, how could I *not?*" Warren hoped his voice wasn't as pleading as it sounded to his own ears. He shook his head. His fingernails were slowly digging a hole through the heavy fabric of the napkin.

"It was horrible. You spend ten years as a cop and you think you're prepared for anything, then it's like God decides to reach down and show you a *real* piece of hell, just to remind you that you don't know shit. The kids who broke in didn't even bring any weapons with them, they just used what they found in the kitchen. My mother never had a chance, and my old man was a vegetable, paralyzed for years. They just smothered him with a piece of plastic wrap, and my Mom...Jesus." He lowered his eyes miserably.

His mom, petite and God-fearing. Had she been twisting in agony even as his patrol car eased past the house and his eyes glanced automatically at the front door? The red-glazed images of things he'd seen in the course of his work—and others he could only imagine—flashed through Warren's mind; he blinked and shoved them away.

The coroner said his father had gone quickly. His mother had taken just a little longer. But not long enough for the two cops to save her after they'd discovered the broken window and forced the front door at 3:13 a.m.

"It's just real hard, knowing I was so close," Warren finally finished.

Mitch nodded uncomfortably. "That's a tough break, man. I'm real sorry." Warren didn't have to look at the young policeman to know the words were sincere.

"Yeah," Warren agreed. Then again, a little more thoughtfully, "Yeah."

When Warren rolled into his driveway, it was already a quarter after two. He'd been only a few minutes from home when he'd decided to knock back a few scotches at Pete's, a little bar in Elk Grove Village. Chivas had always made it easy for him to sleep, though he avoided using it as a sleeping potion unless it was absolutely necessary. Tonight definitely gave meaning to the word *necessary*.

He felt grimy. The sweatshirt and blue jeans he'd changed into at the end of his shift stunk of the decades of cigarette smoke and booze smell ingrained into the old bar's walls. He decided on a quick shower before hitting the bed. He had just enough of a buzz from the scotch to make him ignore his hesitation at turning on the Bluetooth speaker, although he would have never admitted he rushed into the shower after pushing the On button.

The water felt good, hot and cleansing, but Warren's feeling of well-being was short-lived when he climbed out. The speaker sputtered and hissed during the second verse of Procol Harum's "Conquistador." Warren tensed, the towel clutched in hands wet with an equal mix of water and sudden sweat, but the interference faded and the song returned. He dried off and found himself donning clean jeans and a shirt. Without turning the speaker off, he wandered the small length of the living room, passing the open door to the bathroom every minute or so. Listening to the low music, Warren asked himself aloud why he didn't just shut the damned thing off, maybe even pitch it in the garbage and pick up something better tomorrow. He had no answer and for that, he was absurdly grateful. He had vague notions of stepping over the line into crazy because he was asking, then answering his own questions out loud.

The volume on the radio swelled and Warren jumped.

*Car twelve, respond. Burglary in progress, proceed code two, five-six-two-four Glenwood. Time out, fourteen forty-five.*

When his cell rang only a few seconds later, Warren was already yanking on a jacket, the loaded police revolver thrust into the side pocket. He had the phone to his ear before the first ring was finished.

"Hello?" The thought that he could be terribly wrong flashed in his mind like a firecracker; the whole thing could be nothing but the product of his screwed-up guilty conscience.

*"Warren, it's me."*

He felt the air rush out of his lungs. "Yes."

*"They're going to break in—you know that?"* His mother's voice was frightened, yes, but calmer, as if she knew that there was still a little time.

"Yes," he said again. Warren pulled the revolver from his pocket and checked to ensure it was loaded. His gaze sought the digital clock on the DVD player.

2:45.

She said nothing for a moment, as if she were able to see the wheels and gears moving in Warren's mind as he processed information from memory: stoplights, speed limits, intersections. Finally she spoke.

*"I've called the police."* He could picture her, standing in the same kitchen in which he'd eaten countless meals as a boy, the same room in which she'd once thrown herself bodily between himself and his enraged, belt-wielding father. If he'd ever felt there was a choice, her next statement sealed his decision. *"But the police won't be here for a long time yet. And they won't be in time, Warren. What should I do?"*

"I'm on my way," he said flatly and ended the call. He bolted for the door, the revolver in one hand and his car keys in the other. If he ran the lights and leaned on the accelerator, really *leaned* on it, Warren thought he might be able to make it.

He had twenty-three minutes to try.

He burst out the back door, not bothering to lock it as it slammed against the frame behind him. A heartbeat later, his Buick was spinning out of the driveway.

But what if he *didn't* make it, *didn't* get there in time? What if his best just wasn't good *enough*? He gripped the steering wheel fiercely as the car slewed around the first of a hundred turns ahead.

Warren thought there was a pretty good chance the phone would ring tomorrow night.

## ABOUT THE AUTHOR

Yvonne Navarro is an award-winning author of twenty-three published novels and a lot of short stories, articles and a reference dictionary. She writes in a wide variety of genres but favors horror or dark fantasy. Her work has won the Bram Stoker Award®, the Chicago Women in Press Award, the Illinois Women in Press Award, the Unreal Worlds Award, and the IATW Award, among others. Her shorter work has appeared in hundreds of anthologies and magazines. Her franchise work includes the *X-Files, Predator, Aliens, Hellboy, Clive Barker's Hellraiser, Ultraviolet, Elektra, Buffy the Vampire Slayer, Angel, Supernatural,* and *V-Wars.* To make sure she stays busy, she's also an award-winning artist. She lives way down in the southeastern corner of Arizona, is married to author Weston Ochse, and dotes on their three rescued dogs—I Am Groot, Kyah, and Chewbecca—as well as a talking parakeet, BirdZilla.

# Twenty Questions

Jennifer Brozek

From: Attar Enchained
To: Number 12 <slb98052@yahoo.com>
Subject: Hi! Wanna Play With Me?

Situation normal and things are fine. Bored now.
Want to play with me? Want to win big or risk losing
it all?
http://www.aaacdeehinnvtt.com
Come on! You know you want to!

~ Attar Enchained

Sara looked at the email in her inbox and frowned. It did not look like the normal spam for Viagra, money, or the enlargement of any part of the human body. It was probably spam for a new casino. Her cursor hovered over the delete button for a long time. "Oh, what the hell. Why not?" She shifted the mouse until her cursor was sitting on the URL and clicked.

She sipped her wine and watched as a new browser window opened up. Much to her surprise and pleasure, it was not a casino webpage or one of those sites that pops up many other windows blinking and flashing their advertisements. Instead, it was a plain black page with the following:

WELCOME NUMBER TWELVE.
Do you want to play my game?

There was a "YES" button and a "NO" button. She wanted to click the "NO" button just to see what would happen, but she was afraid if she did, something would be set somewhere and she would never be able to click "YES." Clicking on the affirmative, she sat back and watched.

Establishing Direct Connection...........Connected.

Attar Enchained: Welcome #12. Do you want to play my game?

Sara considered a moment longer and shrugged. She typed into the text box at the bottom of the webpage.

#12: What is your game? Why are you calling me #12?

Attar Enchained: You are the 12th person to click yes on my website. The game is 20 Questions. Do you know it?

#12: Yes. I think so. I think of something and you can ask me twenty Yes or No questions. After 20 questions and answers, you guess and I tell you if you are right.

Attar Enchained: My version is different.

#12: How?

Attar Enchained: We each ask each other 20 questions in sets of 5. One set each day for 4 days. I go first. We play until all questions have been asked and answered. They are not just yes or no questions. Also, we promise to tell the truth. It's like Truth or Dare but no Dares. Do you want to play my game?

#12: Both of us promise to tell the truth and the game lasts four days? OK.

Attar Enchained: Great! What do you want to be known as?

Sara looked around her apartment, looking for inspiration. She did not want to give out her normal online name. She did not know this person. Her eyes landed on the book she was reading.

#12: Eowyn.

Attar Enchained: One sec.

Attar Enchained: You're set. Ready to start?

Eowyn: Yes.

Sara grinned. It was clear that Attar was some sort of programmer. She got herself another glass of wine and a plate of snacks to munch on while they played and chatted. It was not much different than random people IMing her out of the blue to talk on one of her chat programs. Suddenly, the evening was looking up. Attar's first question was waiting for her when she got back to her desk.

Attar Enchained: Question #1 - What is a secret about yourself you have never told anyone ever.

Eowyn: Boy. You don't pull punches. I'm afraid of being forgotten completely. Of me disappearing and no one caring.

Attar Enchained: It's a favorite question of mine. It tells me a lot about my playmates. Plus, it puts you in the right frame of mind. Question #2 — What do you do for a living?

Eowyn: Proofreader/editor for a big company.

Attar Enchained: Question #3 - Do you like what you do?

Eowyn: Some days I do. Some days I don't. Today was one of the bad days. Tight deadlines. People yelling. Things like that.

Attar Enchained: Sounds tough. Question #4 — What is the worst way you can think of to die?

Sara frowned at that. It was a strange and unsettling question. At first, she was going to say something flip because she did not like to think of that sort of thing, but she had agreed to the rules and had promised to tell the truth.

Eowyn: Suffocation. It sounds terrible.

She hoped that he would not follow up that question with something else along that train of thought. She was very relieved when he did not.

Attar Enchained: Question #5 — Why did you click on the URL in the email I sent out?

Eowyn: I was feeling reckless and curious. I wanted to know what it was. Your email wasn't like normal spam. It seemed like there was more to it.

Attar Enchained: Accepted. That was my five questions for today. You have five questions now.

Sara decided to trot out some oldie but goodie Truth or Dare questions.

Eowyn: Ok. Question #1 — If you could have any superpower, what would it be?

Attar Enchained: The ability to be invisible at will.

Eowyn: #2 — Why?

Attar Enchained: I want the ability to go places unseen and to more easily watch people close up when they don't know I'm there.

That was not the answer she was expecting for either question. It put a different shade on her impression of Attar Enchained. *Voyeur, I guess. No harm in that, really. Just looking and watching.*

Eowyn: Question #3 — Why did you set up this game?

Attar Enchained: Because it makes my life more interesting. I get to learn about new people from all over. I get to see the world through other people's eyes.

Eowyn: Question #4 — Why did you email me?

Attar Enchained: It was not personal. I bought a spam list. Sorry if that upsets you.

Eowyn: No. That's fine. Really. I was just curious. Question #5 — What do you do for a living?

Attar Enchained: I'm a civil servant.

*Hah! That was beating around the bush. Means he works for the city or state. Most people who say that are something like a janitor or garbage man. I suppose if I was one, I would hide it, too. Ok. I'll give you this one, Sara thought.*

Eowyn: Accepted.

Attar Enchained: Ok! Thank you. I will contact you tomorrow for the next set of five questions.

Before Sara could type her own goodbye, the browser window shut down on its own. It surprised her. However, she just shook her head with a smile and opened a new browser window to begin her usual nightly tour around the net: checking her email, visiting her favorite blogs, reading news sites. All the while, she mused about what a strange and wonderful world the internet was.

The next day, Sara hurried home from work. She told a co-worker about the game and he had been interested in it as well. Unfortunately, when he went to the website linked in the "Wanna Play" email, all he got was a plain blank page. She was afraid that the same thing would happen to her; that the game of Attar's Twenty Questions would be over before it really began. That would be a shame. Besides, Sara had spent all day thinking about her next five questions for him.

She tossed a frozen pizza in the oven and poured herself a beer before sitting down to the computer. Shunning her normal digital routine, she opened her email and clicked on the game link. The black website with the familiar white text appeared.

WELCOME EOWYN.
Are you ready to continue our game?

She did not hesitate to click the "YES" button this time. Immediately, Attar's first message appeared. He had been waiting for her. That thought made her grin.

Attar Enchained: Hello, Eowyn. Round #2.

Eowyn: Hello Attar. How are you doing?

Attar Enchained: I am well. I will assume that is not your Question #6.

Eowyn: *LOL* No. Just being friendly. But I'm ready to go.

Attar Enchained: Good. Question #6 — Do you use Comcast as your service provider?

It was not what she had been expecting. She thought he would ask another more provocative question.

Eowyn: Um. Yes.

Attar Enchained: Question #7 — Are you a single woman?

She hesitated before answering the question this time. This did not seem like as much fun as it had yesterday. Attar seemed more interested in who she was, rather than what she thought.

Eowyn: Yes.

Attar Enchained: Question #8 — If it was a choice between death by suffocation or watching someone else die, which would you choose?

Eowyn: I don't think I could watch someone else die. I wouldn't want to die myself but…I guess I have to say the former.

Despite the unpleasantness of the question, it made her relax. Now he was back to the more interesting questions that made you think about yourself and your morals.

Attar Enchained: Question #9 - Do you live alone?

Again, she paused before answering. Alarm bells were going off. There was something very creepy about the question. If she had been in a normal chat program, speaking with someone she had gotten to know over time, the question would not be so disquieting. She was not sure she liked where this game was headed. Still, it wasn't like this person knew who she actually was.

Eowyn: Yes.

Attar Enchained: Question #10 - What is your favorite color?

Eowyn: Purple.

Attar Enchained: Accepted. Your turn.

Sara could not figure Attar out. Where was he going with his questions? What was he trying to figure out about her? If she was going to win at this game, she needed to know what he wanted to know and figure out how to obfuscate it. She abandoned the personal questions she'd thought of earlier.

Eowyn: Question #6 - How did you know my service provider was Comcast?

Attar Enchained: I looked it up using your IP address.

Eowyn: Question #7 - Why did you ask me about having me suffocate or having me watch someone die?

Attar Enchained: I wanted to see what kind of person you are.

Eowyn: What have you decided?

Attar Enchained: Is that your 8th question?

Eowyn: Yes.

Attar Enchained: I haven't really decided but, on first thought, you're a kind person who tries to do the right thing. Or you're good at saying what you think other people want to hear. *smile* Really, I need all 20 questions to know for sure.

Eowyn: *heh* OK. Fair Enough. #9 - Why did you choose your nickname: Attar Enchained?

Attar Enchained: Good one! Not many ask that. Attar is an Arabic perfume. Attar is also a 1220 Persian mystical poet. Enchained means to bind or hold as if with chains. It has many meanings to me but, in essence, it's like trapping or binding smoke or a scent. Something almost impossible to do unless you are really good and/or creative. Also, I believe words have power. So, I like the reference to the mystical poet.

Eowyn: I really like that. I like it when people think about their nicks. Something more than 'it sounded cool.' Question #10 - My co-worker went to your game site but it only showed a blank page. Why is that?

Attar Enchained: You are my number 12. I don't need any more than you. One playmate at a time. Otherwise, it gets messy and complicated.

Something about that answer prickled a warning in the back of her head. Then the timer buzzed on the oven, signaling that her pizza was ready. She got up, turned it off, pulled the pizza out, and set it aside to cool. She had not been able to ask most of her planned questions because she had been too curious about him and his questions to her.

Sara frowned at her monitor once she returned to the computer, fully intending to sit down to an evening of casual chat with her new friend. She wanted to know more about him than what little information she could glean from the game. Instead, she found the browser window shut again without so much as a goodbye. It irritated her.

It irritated her even more that she could not go back and reread the log of their conversation. She had wanted more time to think about his questions and his answers. Instead, she was left hanging, feeling both rejected and a little uneasy. She did not like the way the browser window closed on its own. Then again, she did not know enough about computers to know what that meant.

The next evening, Sara arrived home late, exhausted from a tight deadline, then drinks and dinner with her co-workers afterwards as a thank you from her boss. She tossed her purse and coat to the couch, debated a moment, then decided on a quick email check before bed. She knew she could get lost in the email and stay up later than she wanted to, but habits die hard.

Ten minutes later, she had finished her email. Ten minutes after that, she was in the middle of reading one of her favorite blogs when her browser suddenly shut down. She was so surprised, she could not think of what to do as she watched the rest of her open applications shut themselves down one by one: email, AOL IM, Yahoo IM, and her journal. Then, her web browser started up again. It showed a black background with these words:

```
YOU ARE LATE, EOWYN.
It is time for Round #3 of our game.
```

There was no "YES" or "NO" button to click this time. Instead, the words disappeared and the browser cycled to the page with the text box.

```
Attar Enchained: You shouldn't be late to our game.
It is rude.

Eowyn: How the hell did you do that to my computer?
Shut down my applications? That's not right!

Attar Enchained: You may ask those questions when it
is your turn. It is my turn now.

Eowyn: I'm tired! I don't want to play your stupid
game! I'm not playing.

Attar Enchained: You have to. You agreed to. Are you
a woman who breaks her promises? I don't think so.
Question #11 - Why were you late tonight?
```

Sara scowled at the computer, knowing that something was very wrong. Yes, she had agreed to play the game, but that did not give him the right to do what he was doing. She was angry and a little scared. She would talk to the company's IT guys about it tomorrow and have them fix it. Game or no game, she did not like not having control over her own computer. After a few more moments of indecision, she began to type. The sooner she was done, the sooner she could go to bed.

```
Eowyn: I worked late for a tight deadline. My boss
took me and my co-workers out to dinner afterwards.

Attar Enchained: Question #12 - Besides yourself,
who do you trust most in all the world?
```

It was a good question. One she had to think about. She got up and got herself a glass of water before deciding on an answer.

```
Eowyn: I would have to say my mom. She and I are
good friends now. We talk all the time.

Attar Enchained: Question #13 - Which would you
rather do: Stomp a kitten to death or watch a baby
roast on a BBQ?
```

Sara recoiled from the computer. Then, grimacing at the question, she furiously typed.

```
Eowyn: Neither! God! That is an awful question!

Attar Enchained: You did not answer the question.
There was no option of "Neither." Which would you
rather do? Kill an animal yourself by stomping it to
death or watch a baby burn?

Eowyn: That's so horrible! I wouldn't do either! No!
Neither! I'm not answering that. Period!

Attar Enchained: Abstaining is still an answer.
Accepted. It was just a question, Eowyn. No need to
get so upset. I was just curious. For the record, I
know you wouldn't do either. You're too nice.
Question #14 - What's your favorite flower?
```

She was thrown off by the innocence of the question after the awfulness of the previous one. At first, she did not know how to answer it.

She looked for the hidden gotcha, but found nothing. It was a straightforward question. Just like his question about her favorite color.

Eowyn: I like gardenias best because of their smell.

Attar Enchained: Question #15 - If you had only one more day to live, how would you spend it?

Eowyn: Assuming I know it's my last day, probably at a spa being pampered and eat all of the good meals I could think of.

Attar Enchained: Accepted. Good answer. Most people answer something about sex. Your turn.

Eowyn: How did you turn off my applications on my computer? Question #11.

Attar Enchained: I am directly connected to your computer. I have remote access.

Eowyn: How?

Attar Enchained: I will assume that is Question #12. You gave me permission.

Eowyn: When? I don't remember giving you permission.

Attar Enchained: Again, I will assume that that is Question #13. You need to follow the form of the game, Eowyn. You gave me permission when you said you wanted to play my game.

*I did not!* she thought, then remembered the message about establishing a direct connection two nights ago. *I didn't know what that meant. That's not fair! I just wanted to play a game. Not do this.*

Eowyn: Question #14 - How do I quit this game?

Attar Enchained: You can't.

Eowyn: Why not? I don't want to play anymore!

Attar Enchained: Once the game begins, it continues until the end.

Eowyn: Then what?

Attar Enchained: You've run out of questions, Eowyn. I can't answer that one today. You may ask it tomorrow. I will speak to you then for the final round of 20 Questions.

She started to respond, to tell Attar not to bother because she would not play, no matter what he did, but the browser closed while she was typing. Furious and shaken, Sara opened up several applications to prove she could. Then, she ran a program to clean out all spyware from the computer. One of her friends had showed her how to use it. Maybe it would clean up this direct connection nonsense. Tomorrow, she would tell her IT guys about the problem and ask them what to do.

The next day, when she arrived home, she did not go to the computer and login as was her usual habit. The guys in the IT department seemed genuinely concerned and told her to not log on until one of them could come by her home that weekend to look at it. It was definitely a hacker of some type and he had control of her computer. There was no telling what he would do with it.

They did not believe she was in real physical danger. Most hackers, they told her, were shy nerds who took on "keyboard personalities" based around what they wished they could be in real life. They could run rings around you in the virtual world, but get them in the real one and they would cave at almost all confrontation that did not have something to do with technology. That thought made her feel better.

She cooked her dinner, annoyed that this interloper had disrupted her normal routine. She liked to play around on the internet. She had a lot of friends on forums and in her chat programs she liked to talk with. Instead, she stayed away from the machine and turned on the TV.

About an hour later, her monitor flickered out of power management mode. Sara watched in frustrated fear as the computer seemed to log itself on, using her name and password. She did not understand how this could be happening. She hurried over to the computer to turn it off but stopped at the words on her screen.

WELCOME TO THE END GAME, EOWYN.
After tonight, our game will be done.
It makes me sad. Let's make it a good round.

Hope sprang forth as the browser window cycled to the next page. Maybe this would be it. One last round and no more Attar Enchained. No more Twenty Questions. He would go away. Part of her knew this was silly. He would not go away until her co-worker purged her computer of his hacker programs. Part of her was still curious about what would happen when the game finished.

Attar Enchained: Good evening, Eowyn. Let's start the final round. As always, I will go first. Question #16 - Did you have a good day today?

Eowyn: Yes. I had a great day. It's even better because it's Friday. I have a special weekend planned.

She wanted to draw him out and make him waste his questions getting more information based on her answers, but he did not.

Attar Enchained: Question #17 - Why did you choose the nickname of Eowyn when you usually go by Sarabella?

Obviously, he got that from looking at her chat programs. It dismayed her, thinking maybe she would have to change her nick. Online stalkers were a pain in the ass. Then again, there was always the 'invisible' option or 'ignore' button.

Eowyn: Eowyn is a warrior princess from the Lord of the Rings series. I liked the name. I used it because the book was in front of me.

Attar Enchained: Question #18 - Is your first name Sara?

Eowyn: If you know about Sarabella, it's not hard to figure out Sara. Yes.

Attar Enchained: Of course. Plus, Sara means
Princess. Sara = Princess = Eowyn. Question #19 - Is
your last name Weir?

She froze. She did not expect that. Of course he would know her full name. It's not like she hid from herself on her own computer. She had been feeling so much more in control after the tech guys promised to come by and help her out.

Eowyn: No. No, it's not.

Attar Enchained: Tsk, Sara. Don't lie to me now.
We've been having so much fun. Lying is not polite.
Besides, you agreed to the rules of the game.

She sat back away from the computer, watching. For a moment, nothing happened. Then the cursor moved to the text box and "Yes" appeared as if she had typed it.

Eowyn: Yes

Attar Enchained: See? That wasn't so hard? Question
#20 - Sara Weir, do you live at 215 Highland Ave,
Kendrick, Washington 98368?

She lunged for the keyboard and there was a brief struggle as she tried to stop the computer from typing the correct answer. What finally came out on the screen was wholly appropriate for what was going on.

Eowyn: YNoesYesNoNo NYesO Yes!

Attar Enchained: Accepted, Sara Weir. Your turn.

Eowyn: What if I don't ask you any questions?

Attar Enchained: That was Question #16. You must ask
your questions. It is part of the game. You
promised.

Eowyn: No.

Attar Enchained: Yes! Ask your next question.

She sat back and watched as the screen started scrolling the demand over and over.

```
Attar Enchained: Ask your next question.

Attar Enchained: Ask your next question.

Attar Enchained: Ask your next question.

Attar Enchained: Ask your next question.

Attar Enchained: Ask your next question.

Attar Enchained: Ask your next question.

Attar Enchained: Ask your next question.
```

She tried to close the browser window, but it would not respond. She tried to do anything else on her computer: open other applications, bring up the task manager, get to her start menu…even CTRL-ALT-DEL failed. Nothing would respond. The only thing that would was the text box on Attar's browser window. She could not think of what to do except to finish out the game and hope he went away after that.

```
Eowyn: #17 - Why are you doing this?

Attar Enchained: It keeps my life interesting. Next
question?

Eowyn: Question #18 - What is your greatest fear?

Attar Enchained: A banal life. Next question?

Eowyn: Question #19 - Who are you really?

Attar Enchained: ATTAR ENCHAINED
```

She was about to type that the answer was not accepted because it did not tell her anything but paused as the letters of the two words started shifting about, rearranging themselves into an anagram of two new words.

```
Attar Enchained: DEATH INCARNATE
```

Feeling numb, she typed her final question.

Eowyn: Question #20 - What happens when the game is
done?

Attar Enchained: You die.

"Oh, God." Without thinking about it, Sara reached down to the power strip that provided electricity to her entire computer set-up and pulled it from the wall. Everything powered down with the protest of machinery suddenly being forced to stop. She sat there a moment longer, shaking. Then she got up, went to the phone, and dialed 911.

A woman answered. "Emergency Services. What is the nature of your emergency?"

"I think someone is going to try to kill me."

"Are you in immediate danger, ma'am?"

Sara heard the 911 operator typing in the background. "No. No. I don't think so. I don't know for sure. A guy online. He told me he was going to kill me."

"But he's not there now?"

"No."

"What is your name and address? I will send a car over. As it is not an immediate emergency, it may take some time. Will you be there?"

Sara gave the 911 operator the necessary information, told her she did not need the operator to stay on the line, and she would wait for the police officer to arrive. By the time there was a knock on the door, Sara was feeling very foolish for having panicked like that. She could have waited or called the non-emergency number.

She looked out the window and saw a tall female officer with dark hair, braided and tucked, standing there, surveying the area as she waited. Sara opened the door. "Hello."

"Miss Weir? I am Officer Belali. I'm responding to a call to emergency services. May I come in?"

"Yes. Yes. I feel silly now, but…I was scared." She led the officer into her home, closing and locking the door behind them.

"That's all right, ma'am. You did the right thing. Why don't you tell me about the situation?"

Sara sat at the kitchen table with the officer taking notes and told the whole story. When she was done, Officer Belali asked her to turn her computer back on so she could look at it. While Sara was doing so, the officer asked, "Just one more question. Why do you assume Attar Enchained is male?"

Sara bent over the computer, watching it intently to see if Attar Enchained would pop up again while the policewoman was there to see it. "What? Oh, because the name seems male."

"Even after being told that Attar was a perfume?"

"Huh? Yes. I guess. I never thought about it."

"No one ever does."

Now that Sara was looking away from Officer Belali, something about the tone of voice and the words spoken made Sara realize that the officer's voice was the same as the 911 operator's voice. She turned to look at the officer, but it was too late. Something dropped over her head and tightened around her throat. Sara was yanked off balance by a powerful jerk to the side. With the thing tight about her throat and the woman officer behind her, Sara fell to her hands and knees. Her fingers clawed at the rope strangling her, but she had no purchase. The garrote tightened as the other woman pushed her knee into Sara's back.

"You know—" Despite dealing with Sara's struggles, her assailant's voice was calm, with almost no sounds of exertion. "—I would have thought that another woman would have figured out that I was one, too. Men aren't the only ones good with computers. Women can be, too—and they pay better attention to detail. Like this garrote: it's a braided purple cord. I know you like purple. I made it especially for you."

The two women struggled: one to get free, one to keep control. Sara's vision narrowed and darkened. Bright sparkles burned on the edge of sight as her body starved of oxygen. Suffocation was every bit as horrible as she had imagined it would be. Worse.

Attar continued to speak as Sara died. "Also, don't worry, you won't be forgotten. You'll never be forgotten. You're my first woman, Number Twelve. You're special. Your grave will always be adorned with gardenias, your favorite. I promise."

## ABOUT THE AUTHOR

Jennifer Brozek is a wordslinger and optimist, an author and an editor, and a collector of antique occult literature. She believes the best thing about being a full-time freelance publishing industry professional is the fact that she gets to choose which 60 hours of the week she works. Visit her at jenniferbrozek.com.

# The Haunting of Mrs. Poole

Angel Leigh McCoy

The Charred Lady first appeared to me on July 2, 1872.

My wedding gown haunted me that night, hanging from a nail on the wall. It glowed in the lamplight and hovered in the periphery of my vision, a ghost reminding me that my life was about to change. I was to be married on the morrow, to become Mrs. Orton Poole.

It had been an exhausting day of forced smiles, handshakes, and toasts. Having been raised in an orphanage in Richmond, Virginia, I was not accustomed to boisterous celebrations with the well-to-do. I had tumbled through conversation as a sea urchin tumbles in a surging tide pool.

Finally, I found sanctuary in my room, rereading portions of *Critique of Pure Reason* by the German philosopher Immanuel Kant. My beloved tutor, Mr. Smith, had uncovered my talents for Mathematics, Philosophy, and Metaphysics, a combination that led him to introduce me to Herr Kant's bold thoughts. I have since read everything the philosopher ever wrote. If the man hadn't died before my birth, he'd have found himself burdened, I fear, with an admirer. Thus, I was grateful for the time alone with my thoughts and his.

The day had sweltered and the oncoming night promised equal discomfort. I opened the window to let in whatever dogged breeze could find its way to me. Poole Manor, my future home, wasn't the most hospitable of buildings and the narrow window granted me a view of only a slice of the grounds. The scent of sweet magnolia rose from the lawn below. From my vantage on the second floor, I saw fireflies twinkling on the bank of the James River, against a backdrop of black water.

That's when I saw her, standing on the lawn, cast in shadows. At first I thought it must be one of Orton's servants, but no, not in such an elegant hooded cloak. A wedding guest, perhaps?

She stepped into the moonlight.

She was deformed. Her features tipped askew as if mottled by so many scars that they no longer sat right upon her cheekbones. This became more apparent as she lifted her chin to look at me. Our gazes locked. I gasped in horror to see she had only one eye, the other's removal having left an empty socket. She made no attempt to cover her hideousness but faced me, as if daring me to see her.

I stumbled back from the window, eager to be free of her scrutiny. As I watched, the glass on the open window frosted from the bottom upward, crystalline and white, spreading like blanched roots up the pane. The room grew cold.

I wrapped my arms around myself, wanting to scream…but incapable in the moment.

Written by a ghostly finger, letters appeared in the frost. It started with a cursive T and my mind followed each developing curve. It spelled, "Too many mouths."

I did scream then and fainted, or near to it. By the time I came back to myself, my sister was bending over me. The frost had gone, taking its strange message with it.

"You poor darlin'." Anna was seventeen, two years younger than I. Anyone of sound sight and mind could have guessed we were sisters. We both had the same ginger hair, hazel eyes, and heart-shaped, freckled face.

She was practical, whereas I had the soul of a philosopher and mathematician. It was always she who reminded me mealtime had arrived or that I was due in the chapel for prayers. I would have starved of body and soul, lost in my books and calculations, if it hadn't been for her.

Anna helped me off the floor. "Have your nerves become unbearable?"

I laughed with her and decided not to mention the woman or the frost. Kant's words echoed across my mind: *I had therefore to remove knowledge, in order to make room for belief.* I was not ready to believe in apparitions.

"Don't you worry about anything, dearest Amelia," my sister said. "All you need is a good night's rest. Tomorrow's a big day." She assisted me with my dressing gown and tucked me into bed.

I watched her turn down the lamp and move toward the door.

"Anna," I called at the last minute, giving in to my weakness. "Stay here with me tonight. Will you, please? Like when we were little? After tomorrow—"

"Of course," she said, changing direction and returning to the bed. She lay her robe on a chair, then crawled in with me.

"After tomorrow," she whispered, "you won't want to sleep with your sister; you'll have a man to give you babies."

We giggled together for a while, talked about how we wished our parents had survived to see the day, and eventually fell asleep.

By the time I awoke, Anna had returned to her own room. I rolled to look at the indent her body had left in the linens, already mourning a childhood in which she had been my one true light. She could have stayed at the orphanage where we'd spent the previous decade, but I'd insisted Orton allow her to live with us. With his contacts and wealth, we could bring her out into Richmond society and find her a good husband.

As I lay there, I noticed a bit of black sticking out from under her pillow: the end of a velvet ribbon. I pushed up on one elbow and pulled it out. Anna had forgotten her cameo choker. It had been our mother's.

I was shocked by its state. It was battered, stained with a dark substance that had seeped into cracks I'd never noticed before. The cameo itself was the profile of a woman, but her nose had broken off. It struck me that her eye was just a carved hole.

Remembering the Charred Lady, I shivered, and it was enough to push me out of bed. I replaced the memory with activity. It was, after all, my wedding day and I had many preparations to make.

When Anna came to help me dress and arrange my hair, I asked her as gently as I could about the choker. "How did it get so damaged?"

Anna stared at it in horror, took it in her own two hands and turned it over. She trembled, on the verge of tears. "I don't know," she said. "Where did you find it?"

"It was here, under the pillow, this morning."

Shaking her head, she turned toward the door. "This can't be mine. Who would do this?" She hurried from the room with me on her heels.

She went straight to her jewelry box. I saw over her shoulder that her own cameo was there, the perfect twin of the ruined one. It wasn't cracked and its black velvet ribbon was pristine. She turned a grin on me. "There? You see? You scared me for nothing. This isn't mine."

She handed the stained and dirtied one back to me. I stared down at it, wondering how there could be two of them, so alike, and yet with such different stories.

Upon returning to my room, I tucked the mysterious choker in a trinket box and put it out of my mind in favor of bridal bliss.

"Are you crying?" There was no tenderness in the question.

I couldn't answer.

"Stop it. This is what you were created for. God put Woman on this Earth so Man could make babies in her. You are my wife now. This is your duty."

I nodded, but the tears continued to flow as Orton, my husband, positioned himself between my legs. I had the urge to shove him away, to hit him in the face and flee, but I did not. I had made my bargain. I was his wife. The finality of it hit me.

"Stop crying, I say. Obey me. Or cover your head. I don't care to see it. It's weakening my resolve."

He pulled the sheet over my face.

As he slid his rod around, searching for ingress, I bit a clump of linens. Never had I imagined it would be like that.

The pain was nothing compared to the shame.

He was gentle, at first. Then his breathing became labored and it was as if a demon had taken hold of him. He clutched at my shoulders, grunting and rutting upon me like a mindless beast. His sweat was pungent and slick.

Then, abruptly, he gave a shudder and stopped. He uncoupled us and climbed off me to stand by the bed. His hands were on my thighs. He examined the space between.

"Well," he said. "It would seem you were a virgin. That is a relief."

On April 14, 1873, the doctor lay the small bundle in my arms and I swooned with happiness. It squirmed, as if delighted to be out of the confines of my body. Tiny pink feet, those that had kicked outward from inside, were free at last to kick at the great big world instead, and kick she did.

"What will you name her?" asked the doctor, peering down his hook nose from serious brown eyes.

"Rose," I said. "Rose Mary Poole. Rose was my mother's name. Mary was the name of Mr. Poole's mother."

"A solid choice," replied the doctor without a smile. "I'll make note of it then." He walked away.

I was drawn to gaze upon the pinched, splotched, gorgeous face of my daughter. "Can my husband come in?" I asked.

The doctor opened the door. "Mr. Poole, your wife is asking for you."

"Is it over?" Orton asked.

"Yes, sir. Mother and daughter are fine."

"Daughter?"

I held my breath.

"Yes, sir. Your wife has informed me—"

A loud crash sounded in the hallway and Orton hissed. "A girl!"

I heard him storm off, my heart rising higher in my throat with every thud of his boots. By the time the doctor returned, my face was hot and flushed with embarrassment.

The doctor averted his gaze. "I'll come back in the morning to check on you both."

Anna came in and sat beside me on the bed. I introduced her to her niece. She beamed, as amazed by Rose as I was.

"You're happy," Anna said.

I smiled. "Kant said, 'Happiness is not an ideal of reason, but of imagination.' If that be the case, then I imagine I am indeed happier at this moment than I have ever been before."

We didn't speak again for a long time, content to listen to the musical sounds of a newborn. Finally Anna asked, "Do you want me to talk to him?"

I knew she meant Orton. "No," I replied. "He doesn't make any secret of his feelings, never has. I'll just have to give him a boy next time."

"You do that," said Anna. "This baby is for you. He can have the next one."

We laughed, until she said, "But I do think I need to give him a piece of my mind. He shouldn't treat you so."

"It's okay, dearest," I tried to reassure her. "I'm used to his moods. They don't affect me anymore."

"They affect me," said Anna with the same strength in her voice that had gotten us through the lean years after our parents died.

I slept on and off between feedings. Later, after the sun had gone down, Orton came to see me. He shuffled in with his hat in his hands and a tight smile on his face. His brown hair was windblown and damp.

"It appears," he said, "I owe you an apology." Tall and broad as he was, he made a strong presence at the foot of the bed.

"No," I said. "You don't."

"Your sister believes I do and I've a mind to think she's right. It's not your fault."

I could hear him skirting around the words he was thinking but didn't want to say. It wasn't my fault I'd borne him a girl.

"She talked to you?"

"She gave me an earful of wasps." He came around the bed and bent to kiss me on the forehead. He smelled of night air, sweat, and pipe smoke. "Don't fret now. You rest. It's been a long day."

I didn't need to be told twice. He had eased my mind about his unhappiness and I was exhausted.

The next morning, the fog of sleep was slow to withdraw. I lay in bed, moving my legs, feeling the pain in my belly and remembering the birth. I stretched and a sudden prick of pain on my forearm caused me to cry out in alarm. I half sat up to see what had caused it.

There was a dead rose lying in the bed beside me, its stem brown and dry, its petals desiccated and crumbling. A petrified thorn had pricked my arm and I found a smear of blood there.

I was certain the rose hadn't been there when I'd fallen asleep.

*Why,* I wondered, *would anyone do such a thing?*

Unnerved, I crawled out of bed, easing my way onto my feet. I ignored the pain and crept across the room to Rose's crib.

Ida, my maid, snuck in from the nursery a moment later. "Mrs. Poole, you shouldn't be on your feet yet. I can bring the baby to you." Ida had plain brown hair restrained in a bun at the nape of her neck. Wisps of it had escaped and curled around her crow's feet and the deep indents on either side of her mouth.

"I'm fine," I said. "I'd like to sit in the rocker and nurse her."

"Of course, ma'am." Ida hurried to pull the rocker closer and to put an extra cushion on the seat.

My baby was sound asleep, her skin already smoother, her little hands curled. Beside her, there was another dead rose.

"What is this?" I cried. "Ida, did you put this here?" I removed the crumbling flower from the crib and held it toward the nursemaid.

"No, ma'am," Ida said, fear in her eyes. "I'd never!"

There came a knock on the door, sober and steady.

I dropped the flower to the floor and picked up my child.

Ida hurried to the door. She opened it only a crack. "Yes?"

An unfamiliar voice, a man with dark edges around his tone, said, "Make your mistress presentable, madam. I would have a word with her."

Whoever he was, he had to wait in the hall for several minutes. By then, Rose was awake and hungry, and nothing else was ever so important. As I held her to my breast, I stopped wondering whether the dead flowers were threats or warnings, omens or mean-spirited commentary. My own perfect Rose drained me and I knew a love more intense than ever before. Whispering near her bud of an ear, I promised I'd never let anything bad happen to her.

The man at the door was a police officer, short and brawny, with eyes as black as the souls of the criminals he arrested. Upon first sight of him, I knew he hadn't liked waiting, but he entered and was as polite as he could manage. I had put on a dressing gown and was sitting in the rocking chair with Rose asleep in my arms.

Ida brought a chair forward, but the officer shook his head, choosing instead to stand in the middle of the room, shifting his weight from one foot to the other. "I have questions to ask you, Mrs. Poole."

"What's this about?" I must have sounded like every other individual whose world was about to crumble.

"When was the last time you saw your sister, Mrs. Poole?"

"Why, yesterday. She was here with me, just after the birth." A rancid unease collected at the bottom of my stomach.

"I see. And did she tell you what her plans were for yesterday evening?" He kept his hands clasped, as if afraid they would wander without tight control.

"I don't believe she had any. What's this all about? What's happened?"

The words rushed from him in a flurry. "I'm sorry to have to tell you this, but a fisherman found your sister this morning—dead—on the shore of the James. All her clothes were gone and she had marks, most on her neck. Strangled, you see."

"What? No. You're mistaken. It can't be her. She's in her room. It's too early for her to be up and about."

The officer shook his head, eyes tight with discomfort. "Your husband has confirmed it's her." He dug in one of his pockets.

"My husband?"

"Yes, ma'am. We found the lady's purse…had a letter addressed to this manor. We spoke with your husband first thing." From his pocket, he pulled a choker—a black ribbon with a cameo just like… "I was told I could return this to you." He held it out.

The choker lay heavy in my hand. It had suffered little damage.

"It was also in her purse, ma'am. I'm sorry for your loss. Ma'am?"

Ida took the baby.

A stubborn part of me didn't want to believe Anna was dead. I lurched down the hall to her room—her cold and silent room. Anna was gone. I knew it in my heart.

I don't remember anything between that moment and when I awoke in the dark, my head pounding.

For the briefest moment, I thought perhaps it had all been a bad dream, but then I heard voices coming from the nursery. They weren't *quite* whispering. Ida said, "Poor young girl, beaten to death. Can you imagine? Right under our noses."

Another female voice replied, "And poor Mrs. Poole, losing her sister so soon after birthin' a young'un. Makes my heart ache."

"And Mr. Poole, leaving the job of telling her to a complete stranger… Terrible."

"Tsk. Poor Mrs. Poole."

I threw back the covers, went to the window, and gazed out at the dark river. The moon had risen. It sat in the tops of the trees, enormous and hungry.

*How had this happened? Anna…how?*

A movement near the dogwood caught my eye. I found myself being scrutinized by the Charred Lady. It was the same woman I'd seen the night before my wedding. Her face was ghoulish, her skull misshapen inside the cloak's hood. A flash of silver at her throat was the only thing that distinguished her from Death himself.

One moment she was there and the next, she was gone.

A burning smell filled the room, the unmistakable aroma of smoke and singed hair. I turned, my heart racing, fearing the house was on fire, but no…it was her.

She was there, in the room with me, and brought the smells with her. She had been in a fire. Given the extent of the damage, I couldn't imagine how she had survived. In truth, I knew she hadn't. Her mouth and nostrils were blackened, and her one good eye bloodshot and swollen. Her skin had shrunk as if the padding underneath had melted. She had no hair left, just ragged remnants with singed ends, ginger-colored tufts.

I stumbled away from her, my back coming to rest against the window frame, and my breath came in small tight gasps, more like sobbing than respiration.

"Anna?"

Perhaps in reverence to my sensibilities, there'd been no mention of her having been burned.

She raised an arm as if to point at the bed, though her fingers did not uncurl.

I looked where she indicated and saw a trail of dead roses leading into the nursery, a garden path left to seed.

"No!" The cork barricading my emotions popped free. I willed her gone with every ounce of my being, closed my eyes, and let all my fear and fury, my grief and confusion, flow out of me into a series of screams unlike any noise I'd ever made in my life.

Next thing I knew, I was surrounded—Ida and the other maid, a houseboy, the butler—with hands and voices trying to get me under control. I fought them and, as my conscious mind resurfaced, a mother's instinct rose in me. My thoughts focused on getting to my daughter.

They wouldn't allow it. Before I could convince them, the doctor arrived with a draught of laudanum. I was delivered unto oblivion.

I attended the funeral as a ghost of myself, unaware of the faces passing before me, offering condolences. By Orton's order, it was a closed casket. When I ventured a query about this to the mortician, he told me it was for the best; Anna wouldn't have looked like herself.

I demanding to see her and when they refused, I screamed. When they couldn't get me to stop, they carried me from the church. The doctor came, with his serious eyes and more laudanum.

The next morning, they moved the crib and rocking chair out of my bedroom and into the nursery next door. I complained, but they said it was for my own good. I couldn't argue, not then. I didn't have the strength.

"I'm concerned for my daughter, Doctor," said Orton. I could hear him through the door. He was just outside my room, in the hallway. I was lying in the bed where he'd first taken me, where he'd given me my Rose, where I'd brought her into the world from my womb.

"My wife has been under a lot of strain and she's always had a bad case of nerves. As much as I hate to say it, I think she needs more help than I can give her."

"I'll draw up the paperwork," replied the doctor. "Don't you worry, Mr. Poole. I know a young woman who has an infant of her own. She has more than enough milk for both. For now, I recommend you let your staff care for your wife. She'll need constant supervision to ensure she doesn't injure herself. I'll stop by again in a couple days."

"You don't think she'd hurt our child, do you, Doctor?"

"When it comes to the welfare of a child, one can never be too cautious. I've seen this kind of thing before. Women are driven by their emotions, Mr. Poole. No man can predict what they will do when hysterical. For now, I recommend you keep her away from the baby."

"Orton?" I called. I wanted to reassure him. I wanted to see—to nurse—my daughter.

Their footsteps moved on, or perhaps I was drifting away from them into the darkness of my own mind.

I had no light inside me, nothing to illuminate my path, at first. Then the flickers came, like fireflies casting their teasing glimmers upon the details of a darkened shoreline. I saw bits and pieces come to light, portions of the truth, memories that gave me proper questions.

It was the middle of the night when I got out of bed and fumbled my way to the armoire. From inside it, I took a small trinket box and found the battered cameo. The moment it was in my hand, she was there with me. I smelled her before anything else, stronger than before; burning wood and flesh choked my sinuses and made me gag.

The laudanum in my blood gave me courage.

"You brought this to me, didn't you?" I asked, not expecting a reply. "You were trying to warn me. But how, Anna? You were still here with me."

She didn't move, just stared back at me with her one eye: so familiar, so like my own.

I said, "Who did this to you? You have to help me understand."

She stood still in the middle of my room, then was gone. An instant later, she reappeared by the window, looking back at me. She gestured for me to follow her and again disappeared.

I was frozen for only a second before running to the window.

There she was, on the lawn, her cloak hanging heavy and still around her, despite the wind bending the trees.

*Should I follow her?* I wondered. She wanted to show me something, maybe about her death. *Maybe she would lead me to her murderer.*

I put on my robe and my wool coat, slid my bare feet into riding boots, and crept down the back stairs. As I stepped out through the back door, she was waiting for me, on the lawn.

The Charred Lady didn't let me get close, but appeared and disappeared like a lighthouse, guiding me away from—I hoped—jagged rocks. She led and I followed, shivering in the darkness, wondering what she had to show me.

*Metaphysics,* Herr Kant had written, *is a dark ocean without shores or lighthouse, strewn with many a philosophic wreck.*

The night bugs were chirping with a regular rhythm. A splash reminded me of the James River's proximity. She took me straight to the dock and its boathouse.

I'd never liked the boathouse. It gave me an uneasy feeling. It wasn't that I didn't trust the floorboards to hold me nor the fact it had no windows to let in light, nor the many strange spiders living in its dark corners. It was more how it crouched there, as if waiting, malevolent and leering.

The ghost appeared at the door and signaled me to go inside.

My skin crawled at the back of my neck and across my scalp. I nearly ran back to the manor, but I reminded myself Anna would never allow any harm to come to me.

I lifted the latch on the door and pulled it open. The rusty hinges squealed as if in pain. The smell of fish rushed out of the building. I felt around until I found the lantern and match box on the shelf just inside.

Once lit, the lantern cast a timid glow upon the boathouse's interior. The light was stalled by the many tools, oars, and benches blocking it from getting into the corners.

The Charred Lady stood in the far corner of the room, gazing down at her feet. She lifted her one good eye to me, then looked down again. I leaned to one side to see what she saw, but I was too far from it.

As if sensing my reluctance to approach her, she disappeared. The smell of her left at the same time and I breathed easier. I listened, but heard nothing other than the sounds of crickets and frogs. I picked my way across the room to where she'd been standing.

Upon the floor, a rug—woven of ragged cotton, dirty and old—had one corner flipped up. I didn't understand, but there was nothing else she could have meant.

I lifted the corner with two fingers and found a trapdoor.

Beside it, caught between two floorboards was a china button, white with tiny blue flowers. It had belonged to Anna. My hand shook as I picked it out of the crack. My tears caused it to swirl out of focus. I held it to my bosom and sat down, there, on the spot where Anna must have died, in the dark, on this filthy wooden floor, with the smell of the river thick in her nostrils.

*Had she cried out? Had she fought back?*

The trapdoor wasn't locked, and I don't know what made me open it—a morbid desire for completion, perhaps, or the hope I'd find a clue. I pulled the trapdoor open and held the lantern aloft.

About five feet below, the river splashed against the wooden posts. The boathouse was supported by pilings, out over the water. I assumed the trapdoor was for loading equipment into and out of boats.

I stayed there for a long time, staring at the black water that had carried my sister downstream.

"Anna!" I cried. But the Charred Lady didn't return.

When I went back to the manor, I sneaked inside, not wanting anyone to catch me out alone, late at night, in a dirty nightgown.

As I tiptoed by the library door, I saw Orton in there, at his desk. He had a whiskey glass at his elbow, its golden contents gleaming in the lamplight. His attention was intent upon papers spread before him. I hurried up the stairs to my room, eager to see my baby.

Rose was sleeping, plumper and creamier than ever. Ida was there too, on her cot, fast asleep as well. I picked up the child and took her to the rocking chair. I don't know how long I sat there with her, rocking, singing lullabies, and chasing thoughts of Anna from my mind.

I awoke to screaming, the kind of high-pitched horrified squeal of a horse caught in a burning barn. It jolted me upright in bed, though it took me a moment to realize the screams were coming from the nursery. Before I knew I had moved, I was there, standing beside Ida, and she was backing away from me, bent at the waist as if someone had punched her in the stomach. I looked from her to the crib and saw my Rose—gray and stiff, dead.

Then I was screaming, too.

The doctor came and I welcomed the laudanum. I let it carry me away on its cloud. Time stretched and warped.

Weeks passed.

My husband came and went, rarely staying longer than it took me to notice him. I never saw Ida again, but there was a new girl who hovered near me, helping me with a body's needs. She said her name was Blanche. She had a sweet voice that could also be commanding when necessary.

Days turned into nights, collecting in weeks and months.

Blanche's encouragements worked their way into my consciousness and coaxed me from my stupor. Gradually, thoughts emerged from the space between the numbness and the emotions, between the sobs and the emptiness.

"You're young, Mrs. Poole. I know it's no comfort now, but you've your whole life ahead of you. I know plenty of ladies who've lost a child and went on to have many more. You're not alone. Your husband's worried about you. You can get through this, ma'am. I know you can. Any woman's had a baby can do anything. God will send you another angel to care for." Blanche went on and on for hours until I almost started imagining she was right.

One day, I got out of bed.

The next, I took a bath.

The following, I went into the nursery to find it barren and cold. All of Rose's things were buried in trunks in the corner. Her crib was as empty as my soul. I didn't cry that day. I'd already cried myself dry.

The next day, I dressed and went downstairs with the intent of joining my husband for lunch. He was in the library with the black-eyed police officer. I didn't mean to eavesdrop, but I couldn't bring myself to turn away once I'd overheard the topic of their discourse.

Orton said, "She's under a doctor's care, officer."

"Mr. Poole, I need to see her soon. Forgive me for speaking bluntly, but there's still confusion about the cause of death. The coroner believes the infant was suffocated. She had…bruising, sir."

My heart fell all the way down into my belly.

"You don't," cried Orton, incredulous, "believe my wife could kill her own child?"

"We never like to think so, sir, but it does happen. Given the recent death of her sister, I imagine your wife must have been in a fragile state in recent weeks?"

I waited for Orton to defend me, to tell the police officer I would never harm my baby, never *ever*.

He said, "She's been acting erratically. But murder? She'd have to be insane. If that's her condition, then her doctor will know."

The officer sniffed. "All righty, sir. I'm sorry for your loss. If I were in your shoes, I don't know what I'd do. Bottom line, if your wife did it—and it appears she did—then she's either going to jail or to an asylum for the rest of her life. I need to speak with her soon. I can't put it off no longer. I'll be in touch, sir."

My legs went weak. I clung to the stair railing and dragged myself upward as quickly as I could. I didn't think he'd seen me, but I couldn't be sure. Appetite lost, I returned to the nursery and collapsed in the rocking chair.

*Had I?* I tried to remember if she'd been moving, if she'd been breathing, when I put Rose back in the crib. I'd held her that night, for a long time. I remembered her stirring in my arms, waking once or twice and suckling at my breast. I'd been awake the whole time, I was sure of it.

*Had I suffocated her—accidentally?*

The door to the nursery opened and Orton stepped inside.

"Amelia?" he asked. "What are you doing in here? Why are you sitting in the dark?"

Darkness had fallen and I hadn't noticed.

I remembered a tiny set of fingers wrapping around my grown one. I'd been laying her down in the crib and she hadn't wanted me to go. I'd had to pry her fingers from mine. She'd been alive. My Rose had been alive when I left her.

"Orton," I said. "I didn't kill her."

"I know," he replied. "Come with me, Amelia." He came to me and helped me up from the rocker, then slid an arm around my waist and walked me out of the room.

"Where are we going?" I asked.

"Don't worry. I'm going to fix everything. I made a bad decision and now I have to make it right." His mouth was thin and tight, his gaze directed forward as if he could see his destination and was willing himself there.

In the mud room, he pulled my emerald cloak off a hook and wrapped it around me, clasping the silver pin at the neck. I watched him as he pulled the hood up over my head.

He said, "Don't want you to catch cold now, do we?" Then he walked me out the back door, onto the lawn.

"I'm in my slippers," I told him.

"It doesn't matter." He kept his arm around me, tight, controlling.

My slippers got wet; my feet grew cold. A brisk wind blew inland off the river, carrying a chill.

Orton walked us toward the boathouse.

"What are we doing?" I asked.

After a few steps, he answered, "I need to show you something."

The boathouse loomed ahead of us. I saw her, standing beside it, cast in shadow. The Charred Lady watched us.

A wave of fear washed over me and I balked. "I don't want to go there," I said. "Not tonight." I tried to twist away, but his arm tightened around me and he latched onto my wrist.

"Stop it," he commanded, his tone dropping into dark depths. "I can't take it anymore."

"You can't take what?"

"I didn't bargain for any of this. I married you, but instead of the perfect family, I got your smart-mouthed sister and a girl child to put me in the poor house. Why couldn't you have had a boy?"

"You're hurting me!" I tried to peel his crushing fingers off my wrist. He pulled me forward so harshly I fell to my knees in the grass.

"Lord have mercy." He hauled me to my feet.

When we got to the boathouse, he opened the door and shoved me inside. I stumbled a bit, but caught myself with a hand on one of the wooden workbenches.

"Orton, please!"

He picked up the lantern and the box of matches. "Dear, stupid Amelia," he said. "I know you feel guilty about the baby. You may even feel guilty about your sister. It *was* your fault, you know? You never should have told her to come at me. She provoked me. What kind of man would I be if I let a woman use that tone with me?"

Orton was silhouetted in the doorway. Behind him, I could see the house up the hill, lights shining in various windows.

I could barely gasp the words out. "What are you saying?"

"Biggest mistake of my life was marrying you. You've been nothing but trouble ever since the day we said our vows and now I'm doomed to spend my life chained to a wife in an asylum. I deserve better."

Orton lit a long wooden match. The flare licked across the contours of his face, deepening his eye sockets and making his jaw a hard line of pure evil.

"Maybe I didn't need to smother the child, but do you have any idea how expensive it is to raise a girl? The fancy party dresses, school expenses, dowry, and for what? What would she ever do for me? She'd go off and marry, and I'd get nothing. A boy could have been my business partner. I'd have guided him, molded him. We'd have been unstoppable." His voice grew dreamy, but then it changed, hardening. "Amelia Foster Poole, I hereby divorce you."

"It's not my fault!" I cried.

"Yes. You brought too many mouths into my house, too many useless mouths to feed."

Orton threw the unlit lantern to the boathouse floor as hard as he could. It cracked and spilled its oil. Then he held the match to an old rag on the shelf. It ignited, flames blazing upward, and Orton pushed it off onto the floor.

"Help!" I screamed. "Help! Help me!"

Orton shook his head. "There's no one to hear you. I gave the staff the night off. Scream all you want."

I backed away, watching the fire race over the oil.

Orton walked out and slammed the boathouse door shut.

The only light came from the spreading fire. It began to catch twigs, pinecones, and other flammables. Smoke rose thick and choking between me and the door. I wrapped the edge of my cloak over my nose and mouth.

The Charred Lady was there, on the other side of the flames, looking at me. The fire licked at her legs. Gray demon smoke curled about her head.

I was looking in a mirror, mesmerized by her, by the cloak exactly like my own.

She stared back at me as the flames engulfed her and I understood. She wasn't Anna; she was me. I was my own ghost.

As the flames leapt, Herr Kant's metaphysical theories engulfed me. I saw numbers, calculations, and equations in the writhing shadows on the walls. In a moment of enlightenment, I knew he'd had it right. *Time works however a person chooses to perceive it.* Imagination precedes Creation. I could imagine myself happy, imagine my spirit traveling through time to give a dire warning. I could imagine myself escaping, and…

I couldn't breathe. I had to get out. Coughing, I bent down and lifted the rug. The heat was unbearable. A corner of my cloak smoldered.

I pulled at the trapdoor, but it wouldn't budge. It was stuck!

The Charred Lady tipped her head back and began to scream.

Desperate to escape, I got my legs under me and put both hands on the handle. I tugged with all my might.

The trapdoor lurched free and I fell backward into stacked clay pots and garden tools. Dislodged objects—I didn't know what—dropped down on my head. I shielded myself with my arms.

The flames climbed to the ceiling. It was so loud, the crackling, the roar—and the screaming.

I righted myself and crawled toward the hole, blinded by smoke and tears. My hand fell through the opening. I allowed the rest of my body to fall, headfirst, into the river. The water crashed into me, then engulfed me.

For several moments, I was upside down and fighting the urge to cough while underwater, but then I felt the slick bottom. I got my feet under me and pushed my head to the surface.

Gasping and choking—the smoke still so thick—I had no idea which way to go to find safety, so I struck out blindly, pushing with my legs. The cloak was too heavy. I unclasped it and let it float away from my shoulders. The current claimed one of my slippers.

I half-walked, half-swam, distancing myself from the boathouse. I was grateful for the river's cold embrace and the fresh air filling my lungs.

A loud crash signaled the boathouse's collapse. The Charred Lady had long since stopped screaming.

Trees on the shore, undergrowth, hid me when I crawled out of the river. I didn't want Orton to see me. I kept to the trees, slipping from shadow to shadow. and made my way back toward the main house. As I neared, I spotted the flaring ember of his cheroot high up on the mansion's widow's walk. He was fiddling while Rome burned.

I skirted around the house, out of sight, and slipped in through the front door.

Kicking off my one remaining slipper, I hurried in my bare feet to the library. My dress was wet and heavy, hanging so low as to drag behind me on the floor and leave a smear of mud and water in my wake. I lifted the hem in the front to keep from tripping and rushed across to Orton's desk.

Shortly after our wedding, my husband had made a grand display of showing me where he kept his gun, how to load it, and how to fire it. I could still hear his voice, "Wife, I want you to know how to defend our home in case brigands show up while I'm away." I appreciated the irony as I loaded the revolver. The act of putting the bullets in their little holes soothed me.

I ceased gasping for breath, ceased shivering.

Access to the widow's walk was at the back of the house, through the attic. On the way, I passed Anna's room and the nursery. My feet were silent.

The door to the attic stood open. I climbed the stairs to the top of the stone manor. The widow's walk itself was a wide platform with a railing around it. From there, a woman could watch for her man to come sailing home along the river.

Orton had his back to me as I stepped onto the widow's walk. The tip of his cheroot created a stream of red light as he moved his hand down to the railing. Ice clinked in his whiskey glass. Beyond him, in the distance, I could see the orange glow of the fire. The boathouse had collapsed and the dock still burned, visible against the black river.

A rustle of fabric, or the smell of smoke or river mud, made Orton turn. His eyes widened in surprise, for just a flash, then his whole face tightened.

"Amelia," he said. "You witless bitch. This could have been all over. Now, you're going to make me hurt you even more."

I looked him straight in the eyes. "There's nothing you can do to hurt me more than you already have, Orton. You stole my life. There's nothing left of me but a ghost." My hand didn't shake as I pointed the gun at him.

Orton took a long, thoughtful pull on his cheroot. "You don't have it in you."

I showed him what I had in me. I shot the walk at his feet.

He took a dancing step backward. "Hey!" The whiskey glass shattered where it landed.

"The next bullet goes in your leg, Orton." I lifted the muzzle.

"No!" he cried. "Wait! What are you doing?"

"I'm destroying the one thing you love best, husband. You." I fired and missed again, the bullet going out beyond him into the lawn. He stumbled backward and his eyes darted as he searched for a path to escape.

"Next time," I said, "I can't miss. Bigger target." I aimed the gun at his gut.

"Amelia, no!" He threw his cheroot at me. It sparked a bit when it hit my skirts, but I was too wet.

Orton tried to rush past me and I put the barrel of the gun right in his face. He dodged and leapt over the railing.

I hurried to look.

He'd landed about ten feet below on the slanted roof and was sliding down it, slowing his descent with hands and feet. Gravity had hold of him and the roof didn't give him much traction. The lower half of his body slid off.

I aimed again and he saw me do it.

Panicking, scrambling to get away, he dropped over the roof's edge, hanging on with his hands. Except he moved too quickly, as he always had. For a moment, it looked like he might catch himself, but then his own weight dragged him free of the fragile hold he'd acquired. He didn't have the strength.

And I didn't have to waste another bullet.

He screamed as he fell...and the sound ended abruptly when he hit the stone patio below.

Herr Kant once wrote: *If man makes himself a worm, he must not complain when he is trodden on.*

It wasn't difficult to play the grieving widow. I had more than enough grief to fill my eyes and heart. The coroner determined Orton's death was an accident. He said Orton must have seen me down by the boathouse, trying to put out the fire, and in a moment of grave worry, he leaned too far out over the railing and fell. It was a terrible tragedy.

Of course, it would have been a shock if the coroner had actually managed to get it right that time.

After the police left, I returned to my room, exhausted. The only thing left on my mind was sleep. As I slid under the covers, I felt something in the bed: a book. I turned up the lamp so I could examine it.

It was a copy of Kant's *What is Enlightenment?* I opened the book to the first page and discovered my final communication with the Charred Lady: a portion of the text underscored. I read, *'Have the courage to use your own intelligence!' is therefore the motto of enlightenment.*

A violent shiver went up my back. I had stared into the terrible face of my own fate—one of them—and she, the alternate me, had gone beyond time to help me avoid her terrible end.

Time had proven fluid and I had noticed.

Inspired, despite my fatigue, I stayed up into the dim hours of morning, putting my thoughts to paper. The last thing I penned that night, though I'd write much more in the years to come, was:

*My life has burned to the ground. The other Mrs. Poole died in the boathouse and now I am just Amelia, not a sister, not a wife, not a mother, and not a ghost. Sapere aude. Dare to know.*

## <u>ABOUT THE AUTHOR</u>

Angel Leigh McCoy writes on a spectrum from cozy paranormal mysteries to dark supernatural suspense novels. Her current project is the *Kitty Kats Around* series of catsitter cozy mysteries set in her magickal world of Wyrdwood. In 2020, she collected some of her short horror fiction into a book called *Dark was the Night.* In addition, her stories have appeared in *Best Women's Erotica of the Year Vol. 5, Changing Breeds: Wild West Tales*—a shifter anthology for White Wolf's *World of Darkness, Pseudopod, Strange Aeons,* and *Necrotic Tissue,* among others. Her publications span three decades worth of overactive imagination set to paper. And…she is a cat whisperer. Learn more at AngelMcCoy.com.

# Glue and the Art of Supermodel Maintenance

Weston Ochse

Ernie peeled back the layer of skin that was her cheek. "Feel this?" he asked. His eyes were wide and filled with the pretenses of love.

She tried to see what he'd done, but the *numbing gel* he'd stolen from the dentist had deadened her to the point that pain had become an ignorant pleasure.

He laughed behind bright eyes, enjoying how she believed it was the feather that he wielded in his other hand. He switched hands and slid the feather along the crease that was her cleavage, following the line through her rippled stomach and ending at the dark patch of her pubic hair. He brought the feather up and smiled as she smiled, knowing she thought his razor was a feather.

A handsome man, he'd been raised in the moneyed splendor of silver spoons, maids to wash his back, and clothes that he never had to buy. Too many believed he was one to throw money around, splurge, friend and fan of supermodels all. It was a rumor he earnestly promoted. Still, the money his Great Aunt had left him allowed him the lifestyle of abandon. It had been years since he'd even looked at a bank balance.

Ernie lay the feather upon her face and dragged it across her eyes. Although she giggled as it passed her vision, he knew she couldn't feel it. Even so, she tried to lift her arms, to brush it away, but her wrists moved mere inches, drawn back by the nylon rope. She moaned, her nose twitching, trying to dislodge the sensation.

He whispered a kiss upon his lips and licked the offending spot. He tasted the seeping blood and rolled his eyes with the happiness of it all. Ambrosia. He leaned in and admired his work, his gaze pausing upon the blood that welled up from the space where her left cheek had been.

Gently, he placed the skin of her cheek upon a sponge that lay on the tray beside him. Atop this, he lay another sponge. Each was soaked in a water/aloe mixture to delay the rot that nature had made his sure enemy. The other cheek came off as quickly, a kiss of *blade-seemed-feather* and promises of love and ecstasy to follow. She moaned with the thrill of it all, never the reason creasing her small mind.

It was her skin that had attracted him.

The chocolate-colored smoothness that had made her spokesmodel for skin care around the world. Her bones could be replaced with wire. Her body could be remade with rubber, but a real supermodel had the skin.

"Kiss me," she begged, and he dipped his head and they tumbled tongues for a time. On his way out, he drew his tongue across her cheek, his tastebuds drawing across the raw skin like sandpaper against sandpaper.

She squealed and wrenched her knees together, her mind unable to fathom the trueness of the act, set on sex—on orgasm.

It was a pity their beauty didn't last—a year, maybe five, rarely ten. He remembered masturbating to Cheryl Tiegs in the 70s when he saw her dressed in a mesh shirt in *People* magazine, pert nipples teasing his pubescent mind.

But like all the others, a year later she'd become passé. The true beauties had only a few years until the hours and the parties and the drugs and the pollution of the world ruined their perfection. Finally, after much experimentation, he'd managed to solve that riddle.

Ernie took her forehead next, careful to keep the character of her delicate wrinkles. He'd marveled at the way they'd danced when he'd asked her to come home with him. He'd loved the way they'd settled when the valet had pulled up the Jaguar. Her infatuation would become love, of that he was certain.

But he was equally sure that, like her beauty, her love would fade and die. Only he knew how to make it all permanent.

Concern suddenly flashed in her eyes, pain seeping through his liquid deceit. He dampened her fear with a spongeful of the gel, gently dabbing, drawing away the blood and replacing it with pain-free freedom.

"I want you," he whispered.

"Take me," she said after five attempts, her tongue as jellified as her body.

Ernie's eyes narrowed. He gritted his teeth. He needed to work on the mixture. The morphine hadn't mixed well with the Zinfandel.

"You will be famous," he whispered, knowing she needed to hear it.

"I am famous," she sighed, narcissism temporarily sated.

Ernie glanced behind him and took in the others he'd saved. Fleeting elegance crazy-glued to a dozen blow-up dolls floated within the shadows of the back wall, each tethered by a slender cord, the helium giving them life. He admired how his technique had progressed. It was the lotion that kept the rotting skin soft, kept them beautiful. So unlike the originals, whose desire for the world to attend coated them in a slimy green aura of need—each, a paradigm of beauty, a supermodel for self-adulation.

Ernie's collection never spoke, never sighed, never whined. Their beauty was pure. It was a rare night that he didn't love at least one of them.

Finally, he was ready for the lips, those perfect lips that a million Hollywood wives craved, injecting fat from their plush asses, fully expecting men to kiss them.

Ernie had designed a special tool, curved and sharp and serrated. His first four supermodels had screamed for hours. Even the gel and the shots and the drugs hadn't been enough. The fifth had died in tragedy, biting and swallowing her tongue in a terror that still caused his heart to ache with the memory. He'd learned that the lips must be the very last, allowing his supermodels to experience the myriad octaves of her own screams.

"Put it in me," she begged, his fingers exciting her. "Make me soar."

He pulled out the stop and rotated the table to vertical. As she viewed her now faceless beauty in the mirror, her lips whitened and began to form a concerto of pain.

Ernie hummed along, improvising his undertones to her terrified falsetto. It was then that he removed her lips and put it in her.

...and the music soared.

## ABOUT THE AUTHOR

The American Library Association calls Weston Ochse "one of the major horror authors of the 21st Century." His work has won the Bram Stoker Award®, been nominated for the Pushcart Prize, won four New Mexico-Arizona Book Awards, and been a USA Today Bestseller. The author of more than thirty books, his military supernatural series **SEAL Team 666** has been optioned to be a movie starring Dwayne Johnson. His shorter work has appeared in *DC Comics, IDW Comics, Soldier of Fortune Magazine,* and *Weird Tales.* His franchise work includes the *X-Files, Predator, Aliens, Hellboy, Clive Barker's Midian,* and *V-Wars.*

# Elle a Vu un Loup

Loren Rhoads

Alondra DeCourval set her carpetbag on the tarmac of the dock. The July day was marvelous, clear and cloudless. Bright golden sunlight sequined Lake Huron, almost too sharp for her eyes.

A man in a red windbreaker hurried over. "Are you going to the island?"

"Yes." She offered him her ferry ticket.

"Just a day trip?"

Alondra smiled at the direction his question was leading. "No. I'm staying the weekend."

He didn't take the ticket from her hand. "Do you have reservations somewhere?"

"One of the bed and breakfast owners is a friend of my family's." That wasn't exactly true. The owner had known her guardian, had in fact written to Alondra about the problem on the island. However, Thomas Lenaghan planned to leave the island for the night, like all the others. Supposedly he had reserved her a room, but Alondra hadn't confirmed it.

"Ah," the ferryman said, "you have family on the island." He took her ticket, tore it partially through, handed it back. "You'll be the only one going over. Sit anywhere you like."

She climbed the gangway. The two-story ferryboat could easily have accommodated a hundred passengers on its hard wooden benches. She was grateful that it would make the trip solely for her. The stairs throbbed beneath her feet as she climbed to the upper level and chose a seat by the railing.

She'd hardly settled before the ship pulled away from the dock. Alondra stared out at the delicate suspension bridge spanning the Straits of Mackinac. It made her think of an aeolian harp, each cable ready to sing when plucked by the wind. The bridge stretched from Michigan's lower peninsula to its less populous upper one, joining the state's two halves and bypassing Mackinac Island entirely. Until the lake froze over for the winter, the only way to reach the island was by boat. This weekend, the ticket clerk had warned, no ferries would run after sunset. Alondra would be stranded on the island until morning.

Lulled by the sparkle on the water and the thrum of the engine, Alondra closed her eyes to enjoy the sun on her face. She'd need her strength to face whatever perils lurked in the night.

The landing dock was thronged with people waiting for the ferries off Mackinac Island. Mothers clutched their children near; kids hovered over cats in carriers or tugged on dogs' leashes. With the sun still high above the horizon, the queue was orderly, but Alondra wondered how the mood would change when the shadows crept in.

An unfamiliar voice called her name. She searched out the man. His hunched posture and protuberant Adam's apple made her think of a turtle, but his brown eyes were kindly.

As she drew near, the stranger said, "I was sorry to hear about your uncle's passing."

Victor hadn't been her uncle, but if the family connection gave Lenaghan more confidence in her, so much the better.

"It was a terrible loss," Lenaghan continued. Alondra sensed that he meant to the world. She didn't disagree as she thanked him. She just hoped that someday she could bear someone's condolences without feeling a knife twist in her heart.

"Here are my keys." Lenaghan put a ring into her hand. "The address is on the tag. Make yourself completely at home. You'll have the place to yourself. If you take one of the rooms toward the front of the inn, you'll have a view of the water."

The people pressed closest in line around him turned to stare at Alondra, taking in her black jeans and black leather jacket, the cascade of jewelry at her ears and throat, and her red, red hair. Someone muttered, "Here's a pretty morsel," to mean-spirited laughter.

Alondra pretended to ignore them. "Thank you, Mr. Lenaghan. When do you return?"

"Three days. Monday. Same as all these other brave souls."

Alondra smiled gently, unwilling to enmesh herself in the island's animosities. "I understand there aren't any cars on the island?"

"That's right." Lenaghan suddenly moved away as the line advanced toward the ferry.

When she caught up to him, Alondra asked, "Can I rent a horse or have the stables all closed?"

"Brighton won't leave the island. He's the one who owned the horses savaged two months ago. He might not rent to you, but I'm sure he can use money, if you know what I mean. Just know that he'll be sleeping in the barn with a shotgun. You don't want to startle him after dark."

"Where is his stable located?"

Lenaghan lurched after the line again before he could respond. Alondra found herself nearly back to the ferry launch. Then Lenaghan turned to point up a side street, past the village's main tourist shops. "He's on Cherry Street. Do me a favor, though, and don't mention my name." Lenaghan grimaced, then added, "Gossip travels fast here. It's the best entertainment we've got. He'll find out soon enough, but knowing that I recommended him because of his money troubles won't help your cause."

Alondra thanked the guesthouse owner and turned back toward the island, ready to explore. An undercurrent of anger trailed her as she walked past the line of islanders abandoning their homes and jobs at the height of tourist season. Better to leave than to face whatever had stalked the island for the last six months, expanding in appetite from pets to horses to a seven-year-old boy.

Better to leave, Alondra understood, than to reveal—or be thought to be the one to reveal—to the outside world what was destroying their livelihoods and peace of mind. She understood the mentality of closed societies too well for comfort.

The island rose before her in a series of tiers. Nearest the water lay the strip of Victorianesque fudge and T-shirt shops. Behind that rose a ring of guesthouses. Halfway up the hill sprawled the whitewashed ramparts of the historic fort, decommissioned after the Civil War and now a state park. Atop the hill glittered mansions of the wealthy: hoteliers, auto barons, and others who had summered on the island before the current troubles began. Alondra wondered how many of the mansions sported For Sale signs now.

A pair of chestnut horses drew to a stop in front of her. Shielding her eyes against the island's flawless sky, Alondra looked up to see the wagon driver in white shirtsleeves, old-fashioned black garters, a black silk vest, with a top hat beside his thigh on the bench. His hair was a sunny blond above sky-blue eyes. "Taxi, miss?"

"I'd appreciate it."

He hopped nimbly down and steadied her arm unnecessarily as she climbed up into the wagon. "Where to?"

"Do you know the Tides Inn Bed and Breakfast?"

"Sure. But Lenaghan's left the island, like all the rest."

Alondra raised the key ring on her forefinger. "I have a reservation."

Some strange shadow crossed his face, but the driver merely nodded. He climbed back up in front of her and clucked to the horses, which ambled onward.

Alondra leaned forward to ask, "You're not evacuating, then?"

"Those fools got nothing to be afraid of." In another era, he might have cursed or spat, but now he only jiggled the reins, urging a faster mosey from the chestnut pair.

The building before which the taxi stopped was grander than Alondra expected. The Victorian-era inn stretched along the street, decorated with turrets, a veranda, and a widow's walk. An enormous lilac bush shaded the front like a lady's fan, its deep green leaves glossy in the summer sun. The Tides Inn exuded a sense of being completely vacant. In fact, the whole street was deserted, except for the seagulls spinning lazily overhead.

Alondra took the taxi driver's extended hand as she stepped down from the wagon. She thought he might let her go without a word beyond naming his fare, so she asked, "I've got nothing to be afraid of?"

His gaze met hers briefly, hard as flint, before dropping to the money in her hand. "Just don't go wandering at night," he advised grudgingly.

"What about that boy?"

"Probably a custody thing, like the papers say. Mainlanders come up here to escape their troubles, but most bring their problems right along with them." He stared at her closely, then offered the flicker of a smile. "You've got little to fear, down here in the village."

"Thank you." Alondra walked carefully around the front of the horses, smiling up into their blinkered eyes as she passed. Then she mounted the wooden steps and let herself in to the bed and breakfast.

The inn was fussy, over-decorated in a historically correct Victorian way. Framed antique photos of the island crowded the little entryway, followed by a sitting room jammed with chintz-covered armchairs complete with antimacassars. The variety of floral patterns competing in the room hurt Alondra's eyes.

She didn't bother to choose a bedroom, since she didn't expect to spend much time in it anyway. The sofa in the sitting room looked comfortable enough. She sat on it, bounced once to check its springs, then began to sort through her carpetbag, tucking certain items into the pockets of her leather jacket. The last thing she did, before leaving the inn, was to rebraid her long red hair.

The stable, scented with hay and saddle soap, brought back a rush of memories. Alondra paused in the doorway, letting her eyes adjust to the mote-filled light filtering through the barn's high windows. It had been a long time since she'd been around horses. She hadn't realized how much she'd missed them.

"Help you, Miss?" a man asked sharply.

"How much to rent a riding horse for the afternoon?"

"They're not for rent today."

Alondra turned slowly until she found the figure leaning against a stall's doorway. The horse inside the stall pressed its head against the man's shoulder. He reached up to scratch the horse's jaw.

The image helped Alondra grasp that Brighton's hostility rose out of affection for his animals. She offered him a smile and moved forward to stand where a dusty sunbeam could strike the diamond pendant she wore in the hollow of her throat. "That's a shame," she answered. "I came all the way up here to discover the whole island is practically abandoned. Isn't there anything to do out here this weekend?"

"Lady, don't you read the news?"

"It's been full of stories promising that there's nothing wrong here, just a series of sad coincidences."

As the word left her lips, her gaze fell on the new stall door across the way. The tone of its fresh paint didn't quite match the surfaces surrounding it. On the wall at the back of the stall—up high, over Alondra's head—was a long gouge, where a hoof struck it. What would make a horse panic enough to kick that high?

Across the barn's central aisle, a gray horse with liquid black eyes batted extravagant lashes at her. Alondra crossed to him, offering her palm to him to sniff, then skritching under his forelock. "Hello, handsome," she purred. "Your name must be Moonshadow or something."

"Moon Calf is more like it. He's too dreamy to be much of a saddle horse." The stable master drew nearer to her, watching Alondra charm the horse. "You ridden much?"

"I grew up on horseback. My mother bred Arabians in Upstate New York."

Brighton stood close enough that she could see the gold hoop in his right ear, the curls of black fur at the unbuttoned collar of his plaid shirt. He looked more Eastern European than the British name that labeled his stable.

"I worked on an Arabian farm on my way through school," he said. "What was your mother's name?"

Alondra hated to resort to name-dropping, but she needed to borrow his horse. "Cassandra DeCourval. If you met her, you'd probably remember."

"I do."

Alondra was used to the admiration that passed through men's eyes when they recalled her mother.

"I can let you have him for a couple of hours, but you'd better be back here no later than four o'clock. Sunset comes before nine thirty and we're under curfew…more like martial law. Anyway, you don't want to run into any trouble with the local yahoos." He pronounced the word "yay-who." He named his price and Alondra fished her wallet out of the leather coat she'd draped over her arm.

She stood out of his way as he saddled the horse for her. Rather than beginning with the bridle, he let the gelding take the bit last, before leading him out of the stall. Alondra stroked the horse's nose again, gazing into his black eyes. Then she stepped up onto the block, hooked her foot into the stirrup and swung her leg over. It had been much too long since she'd ridden, but it all came flooding back.

Brighton handed her the reins. "Normally, they want horses kept off the Lake Shore Road, so you're not competing with the bicyclists, but they won't get in your way today. You'll have enough time to take the circle road around the whole island. That's six miles. It's real pretty on the other side of the island, peaceful, not built up like over here. But be back by four."

Alondra made a show of checking her watch and nodded. "Thank you, sir."

She nudged with her heels to urge the horse forward, bowing her head unnecessarily to clear the doorway as she rode out. The protection glyph painted above the doorway didn't escape her notice.

Alondra stopped for lunch in a shady place overlooking the lake. It was nearly two o'clock and she hadn't seen another soul on the state-numbered "highway" that ringed the island. The silence was almost unnerving.

She threaded the gray gelding's reins around the white trunk of an aspen tree and left him to graze while she sat in the tall weeds at the edge of the road. Black-eyed Susans and purple coneflowers nodded around her in the faintest breath of breeze. A bumblebee hummed to himself as he went about his business.

Across the empty blacktop, waves the color of beach glass lapped gently at the pebbled shoreline. In the distance across the water, Alondra could see Michigan's upper peninsula. Once it had been mined for copper and steel, but now it was mostly wild land. She'd heard it was beautiful there. Maybe one day she'd have an opportunity to visit.

She hadn't been mentally prepared for the distances between one mass of land and the next up here. She chided herself, remembering that the Great Lakes were visible from space. Knowing that and experiencing it were two different things.

She opened the sack lunch she'd packed in the supermarket on the mainland. Inside clustered carrot sticks, a D'Anjou pear, a good-sized chunk of Wisconsin cheddar, and a small jar of peanut butter. She cut the under-ripe pear into spears and dipped them into the peanut butter.

Alondra scanned the waves, half expecting to see an otter or a seal peering back at her. Unfortunately, the water was as vacant as the island trail had been. The drowsy afternoon was warm now that she'd ridden around to the lee of the island. She'd expected that, but she hadn't anticipated how lonely she felt surrounded by water. It was a reasonable ride back to human habitation.

Birds tentatively began to sing in the trees behind her. A pair of blue jays screeched, nearly drowning out the sweeter song of the finches. A robin chirped.

The gelding nudged her shoulder with his nose. Alondra offered him a carrot stick, but he was more interested in the jar of peanut butter. Just as well. It was more than she should eat by herself.

The horse, Moonshadow or Moon Calf as the case might be, was eager enough to turn off the paved road onto a flat dirt track as soon as Alondra found one. He tossed his head, glad to be out of the glaring sun and under the shadow of the oaks. Alondra let up on the reins. The horse seemed happy to pick up the pace now that they'd turned back toward home.

A tingle at the back of Alondra's neck alerted her that they were skirting the edge of the old battlefield. During the War of 1812, the British had captured the fort on the mainland-facing side of the island. The fighting to recapture it had been fierce. Alondra shivered, despite the heat of the day. She usually avoided battlefields. The blood-soaked soil forever changed the vibrations of the land. Too often, ghosts lingered over their forgotten remains. One could spend an entire lifetime repatriating dead soldiers. In fact, one of Victor's friends—bereft after World War II—had done so. As Victor had before her, Alondra preferred to help the living.

The thought had scarcely crossed her mind when the horse stumbled. Alondra thought they were going over and yanked her feet out of the stirrups, prepared to jump. Instead, Moonshadow caught himself awkwardly, whickering in pain. He limped a few more steps, but clearly couldn't bear weight on his right front leg.

Alondra patted his neck. "Let me get down, old fellow."

He stood as straight as he could, flesh shivering beneath her hands. Alondra swung her leg over and stretched her toes to the ground. The long drop would have been an even longer fall.

She walked in front of him, stroking his muzzle as she passed, and stopped with her shoulder against his. Then she placed both hands around his foreleg and gently pulled his hoof upward, resting it against her knees so she could look at it.

The horseshoe still seemed firmly attached. She pulled a ballpoint pen out of her pocket and cleaned away some of the dirt.

An old iron nail barely protruded from Moonshadow's foot. If she'd had blacksmithing gear, she could have pulled it free. Embedded like it was, she couldn't tell how long the nail was or how deeply it pierced. If she pulled it, she'd have to find something to clean the wound and a way to keep it bandaged until they could get back to the stable. The pain from the nail wouldn't kill the horse, but blood poisoning might.

Damn. She wished she'd kept to the circumference road now. Odds were better that someone would come across them there, if anyone was out roaming the island while nearly everyone else fled it. Here, in the interior of the island…

Alondra checked her watch. It was just past three. Maybe, when she didn't make her four o'clock deadline, Brighton would come after her. Or after his horse, at least.

It didn't matter. They'd come far enough from the Lake Shore Road that it was too far to double back. She'd just head south as best she could. Eventually they'd hit water. The island, she remembered, was only six miles around.

She had a long sip from her bottle of water, then poured some into her cupped hand. The horse lipped it up gently. Alondra patted his cheek and said, "I'm sorry this happened. We'll take it easy, but we can't stay out here and wait to be rescued. Let's get you home."

Holding the reins, Alondra started up the path at an easy stride. Moonshadow limped beside her.

Alondra noted the shadows lengthening, but didn't remark on it to the horse. All the island's animals had undoubtedly scented the fear throughout the day, as the human evacuation took place around them. Even if they didn't respond to the cycles of the moon, they had to recognize that this wasn't an ordinary day.

She hadn't intended to be caught out like this. It was one thing to choose to walk into danger alone, but the injured horse was another matter. She hadn't brought weapons, for pity's sake, only charms and some knowledge of what she was facing. None of that would protect prey as large as a wounded herbivore.

The island was a maze of riding trails, bike paths, and nominal roads, none of which ran directly south over the rocky ground. Climbing was hard on the horse, so Alondra avoided it when she could, but climbing down—when more of his weight would rest on his injured foot—was going to be brutal.

Alondra felt as if they'd been walking for hours when they reached an overlook. Between the oak boughs, she could see the village spread below. It still lay a good distance away. The sun was sinking into the arms of the great suspension bridge. Streaks of crimson painted the sky, reflecting in water that looked placid from this height.

A guttural engine revved up, loud on the still air, as the last ferry chugged out of the harbor. Alondra watched it go, wondering how many islanders remained behind, whether they were all armed, as Brighton was reputed to be. Once the boat left, they were all trapped on the island for the night. Were many of the stalwarts sleeping on their own boats, secure that the beast wouldn't cross running water?

Old-fashioned streetlights twinkled on in the empty streets. Somewhere, a dog barked insistently. Other than that, the lack of automobiles on the island made for a kind of quiet that Alondra hadn't heard in a long time.

A sudden breeze blew colder, raising goosebumps over her humid skin. In the east, a spot on the horizon burned with magnesium white light, heralding the moonrise to come.

Time to climb down *now*.

Except that returning to the village proved more difficult than Alondra would have guessed. They had reached the edge of the bluff above town, all right, but the way down was a steep multi-story staircase made of wood. Even in peak condition, the horse could not have climbed it.

They'd come near to the mansions overlooking town. Perhaps the wisest thing would be to hide, even though the houses looked forbidding and dark, vacant for the weekend. Alondra didn't like the idea of breaking in, leading the horse onto someone's hardwood floor, and barricading the door and picture windows. The mansions, however tempting, didn't look defensible.

If the island had been a normal place, complete with automobiles or lawn tractors or any sort of conveyance of the twenty-first century, they might have found shelter in a garage. Even a shed might have done, if she could have gotten the horse behind her and kept it from trampling her in its fright.

She couldn't afford to spend much time looking for a hiding place, especially if the odds weren't good she'd find one. Then her eyes caught on the signpost pointing off into the trees: Garrison Road. That led, undoubtedly, to the old fort. If Alondra could get past its gate, the fort had to be as impregnable as anything. It probably had working stables and hay that she could offer the noble, long-suffering Moonshadow, who needed water, a blanket, and a place to get off his swollen foreleg.

"Let's hope this works." Alondra took the reins again and started down the Garrison Road.

The "road" soon dwindled to what seemed like a path between the trees. It looked very lonely. The clear island air was silent except for the syncopated clip-clop of Moonshadow's shoes. Alondra's nerves twanged as she realized that she could see a little more clearly in the twilight. The rising moon cast black leaf-shadows at her feet.

It wouldn't hurt to pray, she decided, even if she didn't have much to offer as a sacrifice. "Well protected may I be as I roam, beautiful Diana, for I walk with your blessing. May you quench the lust for blood and transform it into love of thee."

When she reached the whitewashed rampart around the fort, she found her courage again. She hastened their pace as much as she felt Moonshadow could manage. A sign pointed to the cemeteries, half a mile away. She hoped to come to some kind of gate into the fort before they walked that far.

A mournful howl ripped through the still evening. Moonshadow quivered beside Alondra. She patted him as calmly as she could. If she'd been alone, she would have made her stand here, with the wall at her back.

Before long, she and the horse reached Saint Anne's Cemetery. Its stone gates opened to the left of Garrison Road. A sign forbade riding horses in the graveyard. It struck Alondra as odd that people needed to be told it wasn't appropriate to ride through the cemetery. She shook her head. Tourists.

The graveyard was only a century old or so, but it shimmered with tiny blue and amber lights. Fewer ghosts than she expected sat on their tombstones. The horse whickered softly, tugging against the reins as he tossed his head.

"If you'd had an opinion about the path, you should have voiced it half a mile back," Alondra scolded gently. "You know this island better than me." Then she promised, "They won't hurt us. Come on. Maybe they'll help."

"What'd you do to that horse, Missy?" an invisible man asked from a tablet tombstone beneath a holly bush.

"He stepped on a nail as we crossed the old battleground."

"That'll be the death of him," the ghost predicted. "That wolf will smell the blood as well as we can. Easy pickings."

Alondra refused to let the ghost frighten her. "We need to get into the fort. Give me directions to the nearest gate."

"No time," the man argued. "That wolf is smart. He knows there's no hunting down in the village, where people wait with traps and guns. He'll prowl the highlands, looking for fools caught out in the dark. If you're not a fool, stake the horse out as an offering and run."

Running was the last thing on Alondra's mind. Despite the sweat beading on her forehead in the humid evening, she slipped her leather jacket on and patted through its pockets, reacquainting herself with where she'd stashed everything.

"What do you know about wolves?" she taunted the ghost.

"I used to hunt 'em," he said, moving out of the shadows where she could finally see him. "Back when the British still owned this land. My family moved my grave twice before I landed here."

The moonlight showed black blood smearing his buckskin jacket. A darker shadow hid where his throat had been.

"Is this wolf your kin?" Alondra asked. "Is that why you're delaying me here?"

The trapper laughed. "I been dead a long time and there's not much the dead can find to entertain them. I figure that watching you run screaming through the dark woods while your lame mule gets eaten will entertain me for a while to come."

Alondra pulled on Moonshadow's reins and led him deeper into the graveyard, where a big old oak spread its branches. On the way there, she stumbled over a fallen limb sturdy enough to serve as a club. She loosely lashed Moonshadow's reins to a tree branch overhead, so that he could free himself later, once she had the wolf engaged. Then she gathered kindling.

After the first warning howl, the woods remained eerily quiet. The wolf was already hunting them. He knew better than to panic his prey until he had them right where he wanted them.

Alondra built a small fire with her club extended into its heart. She kept close, so she could grab the branch out when necessary.

Once small tongues of flame licked through the twigs, she looked at her surroundings. An antique rosebush, loaded with fragrant white blossoms, decorated the grave of Melody Carver, dead at the age of sixteen.

Taking a stub of candle from her coat pocket, Alondra lit its wick with a twig from the fire. She tilted the candle to drip wax atop the headstone, then set the candle upright. "This light I offer to the memory of Melody Carver, plucked from the joys of life too soon." Alondra drew her silvered knife and cut several blooms from the rosebush, stripped them of thorns and tucked them into her braid. "With your aid, Melody, I will stop a beast from preying on any more innocents."

"*Elle a vu un loup*," a voice whispered nearby, its French oddly accented and old-fashioned. Still, Alondra took its meaning: Melody had lost her virginity before she died. Alondra shrugged. Graveyards were more gossipy than small towns.

The horse whimpered and danced, scenting the predator outside the light of the little fire. Alondra pulled her club from the flames and held it aloft, watching for the glow of the wolf's eyes. In the old days, that reflected light had been considered a mirror of the flames of hell.

The animal stood not far away, black lips pulled back as it tasted them on the air. A white mask stretched up its muzzle and around its burning eyes. It wasn't as big as she'd expected, maybe three-quarters grown.

Without warning, it launched itself at her.

Alondra swung the club up to protect her throat. The wolf's momentum was too great for it to change trajectory in midair. It crashed into her, knocking her backward, dangerously close to the little campfire. Alondra rolled to her side, pinning the wolf between her body and the flames.

Its jaws snapped shut close enough to her that hot spittle splashed her face.

With her left hand, Alondra drove the hypodermic needle down like a knife, punching its plunger with all her might.

The wolf yelped. He kicked at her with his hind legs, desperate to escape. Thank goodness she wasn't fighting a cat with sharpened hind claws. Those kicks would have been her death. Instead, her coat took the worst damage, shredding beneath his dull canine toenails.

Wrenching the needle out before it snapped, Alondra flung herself clear. She prayed the one syringe would do the job. She wasn't sure that the wolf would let her close enough for a second shot.

It scrabbled in the dirt, trying to get its suddenly nerveless legs underneath it. Throwing its head back for a wail as frightened as any human child's, the wolf turned icy blue eyes on Alondra. Its gaze had already lost focus. It nipped at its forelegs, trying to bite some sensation back into its limbs. Its thick gray fur shivered as it fought unconsciousness.

Alondra was barely aware that Moonshadow had broken his lead and vanished into the shadows. She was glad he wouldn't see what she planned to do next.

She retrieved the coil of rope from the tree crotch where she'd set it. Tying a quick hangman's knot, she looped the rope over the wolf's back feet and cinched it tight. It took her several tries—she was shaking from adrenaline— to fling the free end of the rope up over a branch high enough for the work to be done. Then she hoisted the paralyzed wolf out of the dirt.

She lashed the rope to the thickest branch she could reach. The wolf panted, its tongue lolling between slack jaws, trailing saliva in an arcane pattern in the dirt.

She shrugged out of the tatters of her leather coat and brushed sweat from her forehead with the back of her hand. Although she felt jittery, she didn't have time to relax. At minimum, she had an hour for the work, if the drug and the firelight held out. She wanted to be well finished before the sedative wore off.

Alondra turned the hanging wolf so his belly faced the firelight. She grabbed a handful of fur in her left hand, twisting to draw it taut, and cautiously made a shallow cut with her white-handled knife.

The fur grew wet and warm in the darkness, but there was less blood than there should have been. *Thank goodness*, Alondra thought.

Despite herself, her mouth watered at the smell of blood. She swallowed hard and kept cutting.

Men shouted back and forth through the darkness. Alondra saw their flashlight beams bouncing toward her as they spotted her campfire and broke into a run. She wiped sweat from her eyes with a bloody hand and kept cutting. *Almost there.*

"Sweet Mother of God," a man groaned.

A shotgun bolt was drawn back. "Step away," another man ordered, "or by God, I'll kill you where you stand."

As long as she stood beside the wolf, Alondra knew she was safe. "At this point, he's only tranquilized. If my knife slips, he'll be dead. So please don't shoot us yet."

"What in God's name are you doing?"

The silvered knife had lost most of its edge. Alondra tore the wolf skin the last couple of inches. A belt of bloody hide, six inches wide and as long as the wolf's belly was around, hung over her shoulder, congealing in the darkness.

She threw the knife down into the dirt and lifted her hands in mock surrender, unable to see if the shadowy posse relaxed. Her thumb brushed one of Melody's white roses, hanging askew in her braid. Alondra plucked the rose and forced it into the wolf's mouth.

The change washed over the wolf's face first. The boy revealed was maybe sixteen, hair bleached blond by the summer sun. His nose was a little too long and straight to be truly handsome. She couldn't see the color of his closed eyes, but she bet they were blue. Muscled by hard work, his bare arms hung down to reach the cemetery dirt.

The men rushed toward her now, clamoring to untie the boy, to ease him gently down to the hallowed ground. Alondra stepped out of their way, completely drained, and sat down with her back to someone's headstone.

A bottle of water nudged her shoulder. Alondra took it, grateful it was already opened for her, and poured a little over the emerald ring on her left hand. The emeralds burned their true deep green. The water wasn't poisoned. She tipped back her head and drank deeply, let the water splash the blood from her face.

When she looked up, Brighton said, "We found Moon Calf limping down Hoban Road as we came up from the village."

"There's a nail in his foot. I was afraid to take it out."

"That was wise. Did he throw you when he stepped on it?"

"No. He was a complete gentleman."

A little bespectacled man stopped in front of her, silhouetted against the dying fire. Even in shadow, Alondra could tell he wasn't related to the others, many of whom shared the boy's blond hair and long nose. She couldn't keep track of the shifting men, but her initial suspicion was probably correct: seventh son of a seventh son. Scion of the kind of good Catholic family that one rarely encountered any more.

"What did you give him?" the little man demanded.

"Ketamine." Alondra rubbed her tired eyes. "It was easiest to get and probably easiest for you to counteract."

"There doesn't seem to be any bleeding where you cut that...pelt off of him."

"I only cut the wolf's skin. The boy was still the boy beneath it."

The first voice she'd heard, moaning a prayer when he saw his son being butchered, asked, "Does that mean he won't turn into a wolf anymore?"

"Never again," Alondra promised.

The men startled her by dropping to their knees. "Praise God," they breathed as one.

*Typical*, Alondra thought. She wondered how long they'd planned to wait for their god to do something to save the island's economy.

"Let's get you home," Brighton said. "Where are you staying?"

Alondra told him.

"Ah, Lenaghan. Crafty old bastard. I'll thank him when I see him again." Brighton offered her a hand and hauled her to her feet. "Do you want to ride again tomorrow? I've got more horses that could use the exercise."

"I'd like that." Alondra couldn't remember the last time she'd taken an actual vacation.

## ABOUT THE AUTHOR

Loren Rhoads is the author of *Unsafe Words*, an anthology of horror, dark fantasy, and science fiction stories. Her short stories have appeared in *Cemetery Dance, Space & Time,* and *Weirdbook*, as well as many collections, including *Best New Horror*. Her Alondra stories have been collected into four short ebooks on Amazon. See what she's been up to at LorenRhoads.com.

# The House on River Road

Bill Bodden

Years ago, a house stood a few miles outside of town on River Road. The man who lived there—Mills was his name—had lived in the house longer than anyone could remember. He had a bad reputation. Cops could never prove anything, but rumors circulated that Mills might know where a few bodies lay buried.

Old Man Mills never bought groceries in any town nearby, nor did he grow anything to eat on his property. The few times people saw him in town, he always seemed well-fed, if a bit thin. My dad said there were rumors that Mills dabbled in Evil Magic; that he was in a town watering hole one night, drunk as a lord and boasting about how he knew a way to cheat death if he had enough of the 'right materials.' Two days later, Jimmy Driscoll disappeared and was never found.

Not long after that, the house burned down mysteriously one night. Mills was never seen again, either.

More rumors started flying. Some said the house came back after midnight on the anniversary of the fire, with the lights on and sounds coming from it—terrible sounds. It didn't appear every year. Sometimes three or four years went by before it popped back up again.

Inevitably, teenagers were the ones reporting it, so the law didn't put much stock in testimony from kids who might have been under the influence. After all, River Road—dark, secluded, and with more than a few good pull-offs—provided a prime spot where teenagers could go to learn the ins and outs of sex. When a sheriff's deputy finally checked the Mills lot out—in broad daylight, of course—the house was gone again.

Then Ken Brown and Julia Nichols—young lovers planning to be married after graduation—disappeared. The cops found Ken's car parked at a pull-off a few yards from the Mills house driveway, keys still in the ignition. No trace remained of either teen. Parents in town wouldn't let their kids leave the house after dark for a while after that.

Two years ago, Lucius McBride had been riding his bike home from a Halloween party and hayride on a friend's family's farm. The family warned him to stay the night, not to ride home past the Mills place in the dark, but Lucius had a paper route early in the morning and didn't want to risk being late. He had a red bike with a black-and-white checkered banana seat. Neither he nor the bike ever made it home.

Kids being kids, they started driving out River Road to take a look at the Mills place, especially around the anniversary, near Halloween. Most were lucky to not be in the wrong place at the wrong time and didn't see it. Some kids had just enough smarts to stay out when the house did appear.

Jerry and I weren't most kids. As we drove into the tall grass that might once have been a driveway, I could feel the wrongness of the place. That kind of chill froze you in your tracks. Jerry felt it too as he put the car in park. He sat there, staring through the windshield, not quite having the courage to get out.

The house was a simple two-story square. Its wooden slats looked half-rotted from rain, mold, and age. Any paint covering the wood had long since flaked off. The peaked roof had a few shingles left on it and a couple of dark spots that might have been holes or maybe growths of moss.

The house had a peculiar glow to it. The lights shining through the windows were definitely a different color: maybe even a little greenish, almost phosphorescent. It was scary but also thrilling and our teenaged, hormone-soaked bodies overrode our good sense.

After closing his car door as quietly as he could, Jerry walked through the grass. Crickets chirped in the grass near the road, but their cheerful music faded the closer we got to the house. The air smelled damp and moldy, like the cellar of an old house. The brick foundation was barely visible through the tangle of dead grass and weeds, a narrow band between the ground and the rotted walls.

Jerry was just tall enough to see through the window; I was taller. We peeked inside. A single straight-backed wooden chair sat in the middle of the room. Otherwise, the room stood empty: no carpet, no drapes, not even a single picture hanging on the walls. The fireplace held only a few ashes.

The sound of tires braking hard made us whirl around. A big powder-blue Lincoln Continental, its headlights half-blinding us, sat in a cloud of dust. The driver side door opened and big, dumb, mean Matthew Ellenberg stepped out, medals clinking on the front of his letterman's jacket.

"What're you pussies doing out so late?" he said with a smirk. Captain of the football team, he weighed close to 250 pounds. Jerry and I combined weighed only a little more.

Jerry spat. "Piss off, Ellenberg."

Matthew walked up to the window we'd just looked through. "Huh. Doesn't look like much."

Jerry had already moved to another window.

I walked up to Jerry, who stood on tiptoe to peer into a room that might have been the kitchen. A woodburning cookstove stood along one wall. The doors to its burner box hung open like a toothless maw. Next to the sink hunched a rusty hand pump, meant to bring water into the sink from a well below. At the back of the room, a set of rickety stairs climbed to the second story. At the bottom of the stairs, an open door revealed a patch of the dark woods behind the house.

I felt a chill, the kind that starts at your neck and runs down your spine to tickle the space right behind your balls. I heard breathing and felt hot breath on my neck. When I turned around to push Ellenberg away, he wasn't there. He still stood in front of the first window. My scalp felt prickly with goosebumps. I shivered. "Jerry, I…"

"I felt it too, Ed. We should leave."

Just then Matthew Ellenberg stepped up, looking over our heads through the window. "Hey, there's a door on the other side!" He grinned triumphantly, then turned to explore.

Jerry held out a hand to stop him. "Ellenberg—don't!"

"What? You girls afraid of an abandoned house?" His laugh always had a mocking quality to it, no matter the occasion. He shoved Jerry back against the house with a thud that shook loose a small cascade of dirt and splinters, then set off at a jog. Ellenberg was enjoying this. He always needed an audience. In a pinch, we would do.

Jerry and I looked at each other. We turned back to the window in time to see Ellenberg step gingerly around a couple of crumbly floorboards. A proud grin on his face, he flipped us the finger with both hands from the middle of the empty room.

I thought I heard footsteps then: the sound you hear when someone walks through tall dead grass in autumn. Halloween was still two days away, but the shriveled grass around the house had already surrendered to the fitful sleep of winter. The 'swish, swish' of slow, deliberate steps wasn't loud to begin with, but grew softer, as if heading away from us.

We turned back to the window as Ellenberg disappeared up the stairs to the second floor. Our jaws dropped as we saw the kitchen door swing wide. It closed with a gentle thump that we felt through our fingers on the windowsill. We started shouting for Ellenberg, yelling at him to get out, but we couldn't tell if he'd heard us.

Ellenberg's heavy tread moved to and fro upstairs, then another—this one stealthier—climbed the creaky, rickety staircase to the second floor.

"You chickenshits finally man enough to follow me upstairs, huh?" Ellenberg called.

We stepped back from the house and waited. We hoped that whatever happened would scare the crap out of Ellenberg so we could tell everyone about it at school tomorrow.

Both sets of footfalls stopped echoing through the house.

Not a sound—not even our breathing—broke the stillness. A shriek finally shattered the eerie quiet, loud and long and higher-pitched than we would've thought possible from the throat of testosterone-drenched Matthew Ellenberg.

The lights went out.

When our eyes adjusted, we stared across an empty space to the woods beyond. A stunted tree grew up along the far wall and out into open air. Our gazes dropped, looking into the brick basement of the house, half-filled with mud and weeds. My flashlight revealed a glimpse of something half-buried in the mud of the cellar: a rusty bike—tires deflated and cracked, with a filthy black-and-white checkered banana seat—sticking out of the dirt.

We turned to stare at Matthew Ellenberg's powder-blue Lincoln before plunging headlong across the yard to Jerry's mom's car. Jerry drove out of there with dirt and grass flying.

The town went crazy for the next few weeks, looking for the high school's star football player. Search parties set out from the empty lot where his car was found, fanning out through the woods and across fields for miles in every direction. They even dragged the river near the house, but except for an old car tire and some rusty chains, nothing unusual turned up. The family posted a reward for Matthew's safe return—no questions asked. The reward grew as time went by. Matthew's car was towed back into town and parked in the town square. People who had liked Matthew Ellenberg—his family, mainly—regularly left flowers on the hood and trunk and put signs on the windows asking anyone with information to come forward.

Jerry and I kept our mouths shut. We were young, but we'd lived enough to know that telling the police what we knew would be a one-way

ticket to the loony bin. Still, I could see it ate at Jerry. Neither of us liked
Ellenberg—he was cruel and greedy and a bully, but we weren't sure he
deserved whatever happened to him, either.

Weeks turned to months. Winter and the snow came and went. The
sleet and stinging rains of spring passed as well, and still there was no word.
We knew there wouldn't be. Jerry kept driving out to the lot, looking at the
half-buried foundation of the house and feeling guilty that we hadn't tried
harder to get him out. The summer dragged on, with a hot, muggy July and
August, and then school started. We had our senior year ahead of us, with
all that entailed, but Jerry had no enthusiasm for anything.

The first week of September, they held a memorial for Matthew
Ellenberg. While there were plenty of dry eyes in the house, Jerry seemed
particularly affected by it.

On the walk home, I confronted him. "Jerry, what's going on? We hate
Ellenberg and with good reason—the guy was a jerk! Why so sentimental
about this whole thing?" I was angry, but also scared. Matthew Ellenberg
had made life miserable for me since sixth grade: taking my lunch, throwing
every baseball cap I'd ever owned up on the school roof during recess, and,
from time to time, giving me a solid beating. It was much the same for Jerry.
My resentment remained a burning ember in the pit of my stomach.

"Because—" Jerry lowered his voice to a conspiratorial whisper "—
because we were there. We know what really happened."

"Yeah? And?"

"And I'm going back there on the anniversary to try to get him out of
that house."

My jaw just about hit the ground. "Are you crazy? That's a terrible idea!
What if something happens to you, too?"

"All I know is, I have to try. I can't get his scream out of my head, Ed.
I hear it in my sleep."

After that, the days dragged by like everything went into slow motion.
There was no question of my not going. Of course I would go. Jerry was
my best friend in the world. We'd been friends since we were five, we got
chickenpox together, we both liked the same music and most of the same
movies. I began to dread looking at the calendar.

When October finally rolled around, time sped up. Before I knew it,
October 28 came. I practically sleepwalked through my classes that day.

Jerry waited for me outside for the walk home. "You ready for
tonight?"

"Yeah, I guess."

He grabbed my arm and turned me to look at him. "You don't have to go with me, Ed. No blame. This is on me. Stay home and watch the late movie. I'll call you in the morning."

"I said I was going with you and I meant it!"

He lowered his eyes and nodded, giving my arm a gentle squeeze. "I'll pick you up at 10:30."

Jerry borrowed his mom's car for the evening. He'd also done some packing: flashlights, a crowbar, and two big hunting knives. His uncle hunted deer every autumn, so Jerry had to promise to get the knives back before the first of November.

The clearing was still dark when we got there. We had some time on our hands. We put fresh batteries in the flashlights and laid out everything on the hood of the car.

Midnight finally arrived. Right on cue, the clearing glowed as the horrible house materialized, shimmering like heat rising from the blacktop on a hot summer day. We heard sounds coming from it right away. We recognized Matthew's voice: he was weeping, begging for it—whatever "it" was—to stop.

We crept up to the window, but neither of us was prepared for what we saw. That straight-backed wooden chair still sat in the middle of the empty room, but now Matthew was tied to it, ropes tight around his chest. His arms had been pulled straight down and each hand tied to one of the chair's back legs. His clothes hung off his frame like wet bed sheets. His letterman's jacket seemed two sizes too big for him.

He looked…old: gaunt, haggard, his face drawn and pinched, like he hadn't eaten for weeks. A sheen of sweat covered his cheeks and forehead. Damp hair clung to his head in clumps. His sunken eyes looked too small for their sockets.

Something else lurked in the room, too, something harder to define. A shimmer hung between Matthew and us. If we looked at it long enough, it seemed to have a human outline. When the shimmer shifted closer to Matthew, he screamed and thrashed. The rickety chair squeaked and wobbled.

Then his voice grew muffled, as if Matthew screamed with a pillow over his face. His arms went taut, straining against the tight bindings, shaking with some kind of terrible agony.

As we watched, the shimmer became more substantial. A sort of milky smoke flowed out of Matthew and into it, until the outline became more clearly defined. It was human-like but very tall, hunched over him, its jaw distended out of all proportion. Its mouth wrapped around Matthew's lower face, sucking the life out of him. His eyes sunk a bit more and the skin on his hands shriveled.

The thing stopped then and stood straighter. It appeared solid now, jaundiced-looking and wiry. Clumps of long, stringy, greasy-looking hair dripped out of a skull covered by a paper-thin layer of skin. It had no nose: only a hole where the nose should've been. Its dry, cracked lips pulled tight across the blackened stumps of its teeth. Its hands resembled nothing so much as a clump of thick noodles, wet and slippery and a foot long. It might have been a man once. Now it was something else.

Its eyes were dark pits. When it looked directly at me, I saw tiny points of red deep inside.

Jerry whispered in my ear, urgency all but taking his voice: "When you see your chance, get him out of there!" He dashed around the side of the house, burst through the swinging kitchen door, and stopped just inside the room where the terrible scene played out. The gaunt man looked up, eyes brimming with something—glee or hunger or even greed. Arms raised, its fingers fluttered, making grasping motions as it slid toward Jerry the way a cobra slithers toward a rat. For a split second, Jerry was that rat, paralyzed with fear, knowing his death was coming but unable to move.

Then his gaze fell on what remained of Matthew Ellenberg. I saw Matthew mouth, 'Help me.' So did Jerry. He lashed out at the creature with his hunting knife, slashing at its rubbery fingers. The creature stopped, seemingly unharmed by the weapon. Its hideous, evil grin haunts my dreams to this day. It lunged. Jerry ran out of the house and into the woods, with the creature close behind.

Matthew saw me peering in and his eyes pleaded with me to help him. That broke my own paralysis. I rushed inside, knife in hand, and sawed at the ropes. Matthew's hoarse, thin voice begged me to hurry. His hair—once a rich chestnut brown—was now pale and thinning. His rheumy eyes, once a sparkling hazel, were barely even beige. Wracked with sobs, he gasped for breath.

As I cut the last ropes, Matthew slumped to the floor. I was afraid he would be too heavy, but he was so light I could hoist him up without help, pulling one arm over my shoulder. I held tight to that arm with my right hand and circled my left behind his back, hooking my hand under his armpit for a better grip. He had no strength left, so I half dragged, half carried him out of the house and to the car.

The keys. Jerry had the keys.

I lowered Matthew to the ground as gently as I could manage, leaning him against the passenger side back tire. I tried the doors and found them unlocked. I opened the door next to Matthew and hoisted him up. He flopped halfway into the back seat, one arm on the floor. His chest wasn't moving at all. I put fingers to his throat and felt for a pulse. There was none.

I heard the pounding of running feet. Jerry sprinted past, followed by a misty gray streak. I heard a jingling sound as Jerry threw the car keys at me. He had always been a fast runner. Now he was being put to the test.

I looked down at Matthew Ellenberg. His face, almost peaceful now, stood in stark contrast to the sheer terror that had gripped his features only minutes before. He remained gaunt, but some color had returned to his cheeks. If we took him back now, we would have lots of questions to answer—questions for which we had no possible answers to give.

I gently laid Matthew down on the ground, a few feet away from the car. I crossed his arms over his chest and brushed his lank hair away from his sweat-sheened forehead.

Jerry was back, still running. "Go!" he screamed. I watched as he ran straight to the house and went back inside, followed by that gray streak. As I heard the door slam, the lights went out. The house disappeared.

I fished the keys out of the grass, got in the car, and stepped on the gas.

Matthew Ellenberg's family was relieved to have closure, but the police report kept mysteriously silent on the condition of the body. A boy of seventeen appearing more like a man of eighty is a challenge to explain. His funeral was well attended, but in their grief, few remarked on the disappearance of Jerry Conway.

Jerry's family had been shocked to wake up the next morning with their car parked in front of the house, but no Jerry. Jerry had been careful, saying only that he was going out, not with whom or where. I had done the same.

With a second disappearance in as many years, the police finally poked around the Mills property for real. They dug out the mud in the cellar and found Lucius McBride's bike, along with his body and the remains and a few decaying personal effects of more than thirty-seven other people, more than a dozen of whom were kids. They didn't find Jerry's body, but they did find his uncle's hunting knife.

After that, the township had the entire place bulldozed. The lot became a dump for used concrete slabs from various road repair projects in town.

So here I am, several years later, back at the Mills property. The house stopped coming back finally and no one knows why, but on a particular October evening, if you're in just the right place at the right time of night, you might hear the sound of someone running, followed by another swishing through the long grass, with no one to be seen. I like to think that Jerry made things tough for Old Man Mills, that Mills—or whatever that thing was—didn't have the mojo left to bring his house back 'cause he was too busy trying to catch his next meal. His last meal.

Jerry took one for the whole town that night and forever after.

I miss him.

## ABOUT THE AUTHOR

Bill Bodden has been writing professionally since 2003 and has an extensive catalog of work in the tabletop gaming field, including contributions to *Vampire: The Masquerade 20th Anniversary* series, *Achtung! Cthulhu* (a World War Two/Cthulhu Mythos mash-up), and *Warhammer Fantasy Roleplay*. More recently, Bill has turned his hand to fiction, contributing to several anthologies including some gaming-related stories. Bill makes his home in Wisconsin with his wife, two cats, and an avalanche-waiting-to-happen of books and games. Check out his website, where he blogs irregularly: BillBodden.com.

# Editor's Note

If you enjoyed this book, please consider leaving a review. Even a sentence or two or something as simple as awarding stars on Amazon, Barnes & Noble, Smashwords, or Goodreads will help other people find this book.

Not only do reviews help sell books, they inspire author to continue writing.

Thank you!

# The *Wily Writers Presents* Anthology Series

## Tales of Dread
edited by Lisa Morton

## Tales of Nightmares
edited by Loren Rhoads

## Tales of Evil
edited by Angel Leigh McCoy
and Alison J. McKenzie

## Tales of Darkness
edited by Yvonne Navarro

## Tales of Foreboding
edited by E.S. Magill
and Bill Bodden

## Tales of Shadows
edited by Weston Ochse

# UNSAFE WORDS by Loren Rhoads

## AVAILABLE on AMAZON, BARNES&NOBLE, BOOKSHOP.ORG, INDIEBOUND

**Also available from Loren Rhoads:**

Alondra's Experiments

Lost Angels & Angelus Rose: the As Above, So Below duo

The Dangerous Type: first in the Templars trilogy

This Morbid Life: Essays

199 Cemeteries to See Before You Die

Wish You Were Here: Adventures in Cemetery Travel

SIGN UP FOR LOREN'S
MONTHLY NEWSLETTER AT

www.lorenrhoads.com

# Coming Summer 2022

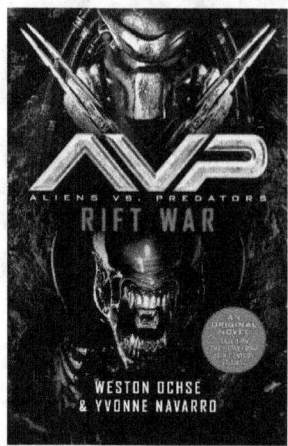

Cozy mysteries for cat lovers!

Learn more at AngelMcCoy.com!

www.ingramcontent.com/pod-product-compliance
Lightning Source LLC
Chambersburg PA
CBHW060439130626
46555CB00005B/2426